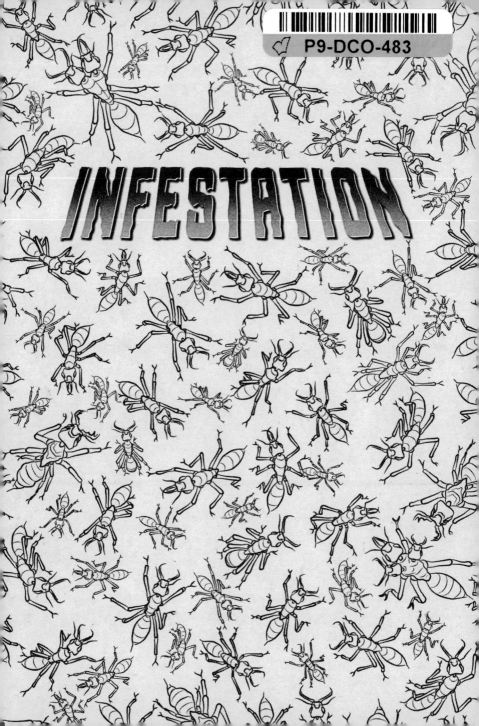

INFESTATION

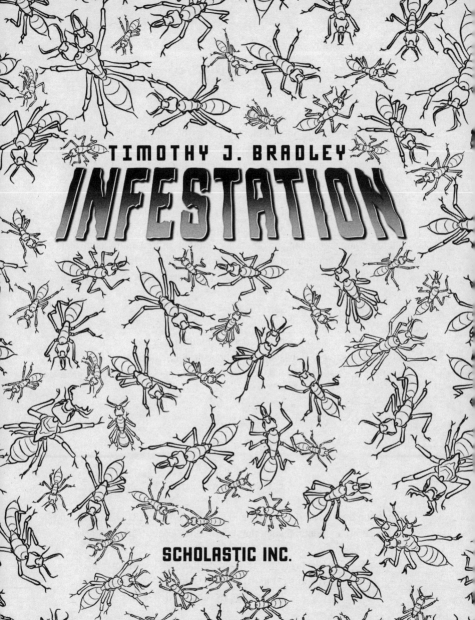

TIMOTHY J. BRADLEY

INFESTATION

SCHOLASTIC INC.

For Kayellen and Ryan

ISBN 978-0-545-45904-4

12 11 10 9 8 7 6 5 4 3 2 1   13 14 15 16 17 18/0

Printed in the U.S.A.   40
First printing, April 2013

Photo on front cover (footprints) and pages 178, 180, 181, 182, 183, and 186 (handprints, thumbprints) copyright © Hal_P/Shutterstock

The display type was set in Berthold City, Medium.
The text type was set in ITC Franklin Gothic, Book Condensed.
Book design by Nina Goffi

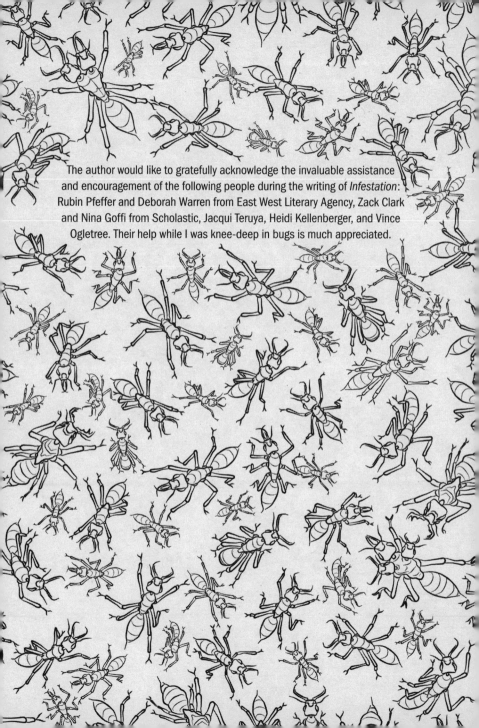

The author would like to gratefully acknowledge the invaluable assistance and encouragement of the following people during the writing of *Infestation*: Rubin Pfeffer and Deborah Warren from East West Literary Agency, Zack Clark and Nina Goffi from Scholastic, Jacqui Teruya, Heidi Kellenberger, and Vince Ogletree. Their help while I was knee-deep in bugs is much appreciated.

PROLOGUE

THE NEW MEXICO SUMMER MORNING dawned hot and bright, the sun blasting the barren landscape. By afternoon, temperatures would hit over one hundred degrees, causing creatures to hide in the shade, sleeping away the hottest hours of the day.

High above the rapidly heating dirt, rock, and scrubby brush, a vulture circled, riding the heated air that rose from the earth. Occasionally, the large bird skimmed close to the ground, searching for the gases released by an animal carcass.

The vulture's keen eyesight spotted a lizard carcass on a flat rock. It swooped in low and flapped to a clumsy landing, hopping a few steps to stop its momentum.

It looked around for signs of any movement as it hopped closer to the carcass. A Gila monster had been killed and ripped apart. Bits of beaded, scaly skin had been peeled back from its skeleton and now littered the rock. Its rib cage had been cracked open, its bones splintered and broken.

The turkey vulture cocked its head to get a better look. There wasn't much left worth eating, but it would do until it was cool enough to hunt again.

It had just dipped its featherless head down to tear at some gristle when it heard a buzzing, chirping sound. It looked around, wings half spread to bolt for the safety of the sky if necessary.

Nothing.

As it went back to its breakfast, a blur of motion flashed over the rock.

In a flurry of razor-sharp, chitinous claws, the vulture was gone. A few stray feathers spinning in the hot breeze and warm blood spattered on the rocks were all that was left of the unlucky bird.

1

FIVE HOURS INTO THE DRIVE THROUGH the desolate New Mexico wasteland, twelve-year-old Andy Greenwood was convinced that nothing could survive here. The only moving thing he'd spotted so far was a dust devil swirling across the cracked highway.

The tired old bus that carried Andy and ten other boys was struggling to keep the temperature inside bearable. The air was clammy and lukewarm, but better than the heat Andy could feel radiating through the scratched, cloudy bus window when he placed his palm against it.

Andy sat near the back of the bus. As he turned from the window and looked forward, he could see that most of the other boys were sleeping. A couple of them were staring, unseeing, out the hazy windows, or at the floor.

A high chain-link fence came into view, running beside the road. After driving along it for a few minutes, the bus turned off the broken blacktop highway onto a darker paved road that led away from the highway. Andy could see what looked like a building at the end of the road.

A large sign was mounted on the fence. It had been painted bright white. Black letters spelled out THE RECLA-MATION SCHOOL FOR BOYS, INC. Underneath was written: WE PUT BOYS BACK ON THE RIGHT TRACK! There was more, but they passed the sign before Andy was able to read what it said.

A group of low buildings came into view. They were windowless cement blocks painted gray. The paint had faded and chipped from being exposed to the harsh conditions. The place looked less like a school than an abandoned factory where atomic bombs had been constructed.

The bus pulled into a seamed and patched circular drive in front of a building marked 1A, and creaked to a stop. The driver opened the doors and exited the bus without a word.

A big man climbed up into the bus. He was holding a clipboard and was dressed in a dark blue polo shirt and baseball cap, both embroidered with the logo of the school, a cheerful sun shining down on a road. The man flipped through a couple of sheets of paper and looked at the eleven kids on the bus.

"Welcome to the Reclamation School. My name is Maxwell. I'm in charge of security. You all know why you're on this bus, but I'll just take a minute to remind you fine, upstanding young men. You are here because the traditional state and local programs weren't effective in your particular cases. They don't know what to do with you. We do. A word of advice: If you screw up here, the next step is juvenile hall. Jail for kids. Do what you're told, and we'll all get along just fine.

"All right, everyone off the bus, and I'll get you checked in."

The boys stood up and shuffled off the bus, giving their names and paperwork to Maxwell. He led them to a large entrance and held the metal door open as he watched the boys file inside.

They walked down a corridor that had once been painted a bright yellow. It was warm and humid inside the hallway. Large posters of happy boys playing base-ball, studying, and posing with pleasant-looking moms and dads lined the hallway. Each poster had some kind of caption: *The Right Track Means a Bright Future. Be a Productive Citizen — Stay on the Right Track!* All had the Reclamation School for Boys, Inc. logo printed at the bottom. Many of the posters were starting to curl from the humidity, their edges moldy and discolored.

The boy next to Andy snorted. Another muttered, "You gotta be kidding," under his breath.

A sharp *whack* made the boys jump. Maxwell slammed the clipboard against the wall again. Something fell to the floor. It was some kind of bug, its legs kicking feebly.

"You little . . ." Maxwell muttered. The bug crunched under his shoe. He looked back. "Let's continue, ladies."

Maxwell led them into a classroom-sized area, empty except for several rows of plastic chairs.

He gestured and said, "Have a seat. You'll each have a brief meeting with the headmaster before going to your rooms. Abercrombie, you're up first."

The boy who had snorted at the posters in the hallway followed Maxwell out of the room.

The rest of the boys sat down and slumped in their seats, alone with their thoughts once again. Andy sat in a chair against the wall, giving him a view of the rest of the room, and the doorway. The warm, sticky air sucked all the energy out of him, and his mind drifted.

Andy had been sentenced to spend three months at the Reclamation School for running away from the four foster homes he'd been sent to over the last eighteen months. At the last one, in Arizona, the drunken foster father had hit the mother a couple of times. Andy had tried to stop it once, and the guy backhanded him, knocking Andy (and one of his teeth) to the floor. Andy wanted more than anything to take a swing at him, but he was just too small; the guy was taller and outweighed Andy by about one hundred pounds, most of it carried in his beer gut.

Andy, furious, swore to himself that he would even the score. His mouth throbbed where his tooth had been knocked out. As he rubbed it absently, his mind started to piece together a plan.

The next night, around three a.m., Andy snuck out to the ramshackle garage attached to the sagging single-story house. Chazz, the foster father, liked working on cars. He was restoring a 1969 Pontiac LeMans and an old Harley he tooled around town with. Andy tiptoed through the darkened house and took the keys to both from the kitchen hook once he was sure that Chazz had passed out, snoring, on the living room floor in front of the television. Andy peered around the kitchen corner into the living room. Wanda Sue had retreated back to their bedroom, most likely reading one of her trashy romance novels.

Andy didn't turn on the lights in the garage, but used a little flashlight that was always on the kitchen counter (necessary because Chazz and his wife, Wanda Sue, frequently got behind on the electric bill). He switched it on and made his way carefully around. Toolboxes and mechanical junk made the garage into a maze. He checked out the Harley first. He inserted the key into the ignition with shaking hands and turned it until the accessory lights blinked on. It looked like it had a half tank of gas. The fury he'd felt the night before had burned away, leaving only a sick certainty that Chazz would kill him if he didn't get moving.

He opened the garage door slowly. It creaked as it started moving and almost lifted him off the ground as it swung upward. It was quiet outside. The only sound was the leaves gently rustling in the cool night breeze.

The LeMans was a faded gold, with a huge hood scoop and a big spoiler mounted on the trunk. Chazz loved this car, and he spent almost all his spare time working on it. When it was finished, it would be an impressive car to show off to the other guys living on the dead-end street.

Andy grabbed an empty plastic container and an adjustable wrench, and slid underneath the car, using the flashlight to locate the oil-pan plug. He pulled the plastic bucket right underneath the oil pan and unscrewed the plug, grunting with the effort to loosen it. Thick motor oil started to pour out, like blood from a severed artery. Once the oil stopped dripping, he scrambled out from under the car, carefully pulling the container filled with oil after him. *Don't want to waste a drop*, he thought crazily.

He opened the door and sat in the driver's seat for a moment. It was a shame. It really was a nice car. When he turned the ignition key, the engine cranked over and started up smoothly. Andy gunned the engine a couple of times to get it warmed up as quickly as he could.

Running with no oil would be fatal for it. The engine would melt into a useless block of metal.

He climbed out, leaving the door open, and went over to the nearby motorcycle. He turned the key and it chugged to life. Andy picked up his knapsack and slung it over his shoulder.

He hesitated for a moment. Up to this point, he could stop. Turn off the engine and go back to bed, no harm done.

His throbbing jaw reminded him of Chazz's drunken rage, and Andy upended the bucket into the car. Oil splashed over everything, staining the beige leather bucket seats with the thick, sticky fluid.

He tossed the empty container into the car and jumped on the motorcycle. He wanted to put some distance between himself and this place before his retaliation was discovered. He eased the clutch out and turned the throttle enough to get the bike moving. The kickstand popped up, and he scooted down the driveway, almost losing control as he turned onto the street. This motor-cycle was bigger than the dirt bikes he'd been riding for years, but if he was careful, he would stay in control.

He picked up speed as he drove through the darkened Arizona night. He would need to ditch the bike and hitch a ride somewhere before it got too hot. But right now, he didn't want to think. His mood was lifted by the night breeze. The empty highway stretched out before him into the dark. *Anything* could be out there.

The police caught up with him about two hours later. His destruction of the LeMans's engine had been discovered and phoned in. It wasn't too difficult to track him down. When he was pulled over, he kicked the motorcycle down the embankment on the side of the highway before the highway patrol officer could reach him.

Thanks for the ride, Chazz, he thought as he watched the heavy bike roll and bump down the embankment. The cloud of dust it raised turned blue and red from the police cruiser's lights.

"Greenwood . . . *Greenwood.*"

Andy looked up. He had been lost in thought. He raised his hand a little bit to indicate that he'd heard.

"Let's go," Maxwell rumbled.

Andy stood and followed, his sweaty T-shirt sticking to

his back. He looked around the room as he left and realized that most of the boys had been processed already. He was one of the last ones left.

He followed Maxwell down several corridors and ended up in a small sitting area with a receptionist's desk. Just beyond were a set of large wooden doors with that Reclamation School, Inc. logo displayed in stained glass as if it were some kind of holy design.

A severe-looking old lady sat at the desk. Her hair was wilting because of the heat. Maxwell said, "Okay, Mrs. Frost, here's Greenwood for the headmaster."

Mrs. Frost nodded, and touched a key on an intercom. The large doors buzzed for a moment. "Thank you, Mr. Maxwell. Master Greenwood may go in." She looked at Andy briefly, as if he were an interesting species of bug.

"Well, what are you waiting for? The headmaster is a busy man. Get moving," Maxwell said.

Andy walked slowly to the doors, and pushed them open. He thought, *Three months will go by fast. Three months will go by fast. Three months will go by fast.*

IT'S FREEZING IN HERE! **ANDY THOUGHT** to himself. A large air-conditioning unit blasted out a constant chilly breeze from a corner window. He shivered slightly.

The headmaster's office was clean and very neat: no clutter on the desk, save for a couple of manila folders and an old lamp with a stained-glass lampshade. Dragonflies made out of colored glass shards decorated the shade. There was an old computer monitor on the desk, as well as a chunky phone. A can of bug spray was sitting at the edge of the desk, looking out of place. The black, segmented chair behind the desk looked to Andy like the shell of a huge beetle. The walls were freshly painted battleship gray.

Hanging on the walls were awards and diplomas, along with some of those Reclamation School, Inc. motivational posters. Everything was faded from the constant sunlight beaming through the windows.

"Sit down, Master Greenwood." A voice came from behind him. Andy turned and saw a small, thin man, who had to be at least sixty. He wore a dark suit with a dark red tie. A pair of frameless glasses magnified his eyes. The man was completely bald, with blue veins under his pink, paper-thin skin. There were some nasty-looking red bites or welts on the top of his head.

He took a seat as Maxwell left the room. The man sat down behind his desk and tapped at the computer for a moment. He studied the monitor and turned to Andy with a chilly smile.

"Welcome to the Reclamation School, Master Greenwood. I am Joseph Switch, the headmaster of this facility, which is the first of its kind.

"The Reclamation School is an experiment started about four years ago by myself, to address a growing need. More and more young people every year are leaving the educational system in this country. Some leave voluntarily, some are expelled. My approach is to combine a private school and correctional facility to see if my methods for getting boys 'back on track' are effective. So far, the results have been astounding. I'm very keen to expand, and very protective of how things are run here.

"The building itself is also interesting. Before we took ownership of it, it was some sort of a government defense laboratory." Switch pronounced it *lah-BORE-ah-tree*.

"We still have a good bit of work to do to the buildings, but they are adequate for the moment. For now, most of the classrooms are empty, and locked."

He glanced again at the computer monitor, scratching absentmindedly at a red welt on his neck, just above his shirt collar.

"I've only looked at your file briefly: parents killed two years ago . . . no other close family, sent to four foster homes. You ran away from all four, the last after vandalizing a car and stealing a motorcycle. Your caseworker contacted us regarding your case. The judge at your juvenile hearing recommended three months here. We'll see. We have a very . . . *flexible* approach to a boy's stay here at Reclamation. If you spend your time here wisely, are diligent in your studies, and stay out of trouble, your stay may be shortened. If not, your stay will be longer. Possibly much, *much* longer. Our relationship with the court system allows *us* to decide when one of our boys is ready to either reenter society or be remanded to juvenile detention."

Andy kept his face expressionless, but as if he were reading Andy's thoughts, Switch said, "You may be thinking that you will be able to run away from here as easily as you did your foster homes. That may be true, although I like to think that the security measures here are adequate. However, let's assume that you were able to leave the Reclamation School complex. Where would you go? We are sitting several hours by car from the nearest town. Without several days' supply of food and, more important, water, you wouldn't last long in this heat. I've heard that dying of thirst is extremely unpleasant. Our first year in this facility, several boys did just that. Unfortunately, we were not able to locate them in time." He shook his head sadly. "A shame." One side of the headmaster's mouth twisted up in a smirk, but his eyes remained cold and hard behind his thick eyeglasses.

Andy gulped.

Switch stood up, and pressed a button on his desk. The office door opened, and Maxwell gestured him out.

As Andy left the office, Switch said, "I'm sure you'll do just fine here, Master Greenwood. Just *fine*."

He gave Andy a yellow-toothed smile that sent a nervous shiver down Andy's spine.

After a quick dinner served in a small, windowless room, Maxwell took Andy and the rest of the group of boys he came in with to a storeroom, where they all received blankets, some extra T-shirts, and bright yellow baseball caps. Everything had the Reclamation School logo stitched or printed on it.

"Greenwood. You're in here," Maxwell said. They had stopped in front of Room 073. Maxwell opened the door onto one of the small rooms. "Porter! You have a new roommate."

Something shifted in the top bunk bed along the wall. A blond head with huge eyes looked over the top of the pillow warily.

Maxwell nudged Andy into the room and said, "Lights out in thirty minutes. Porter, show Greenwood where the bathroom is, and where he can stow his stuff." He closed the door, leaving the two boys in an uneasy silence.

The boy named Porter jumped off the top bunk, and regarded Andy with suspicion. He was a few inches shorter than Andy and very thin, with spindly arms and legs. There were dark circles under his eyes, giving him a haunted look. He scratched at a red welt on the back of his hand.

"Hi," Andy said. "I'm Andy." He extended his hand.

The boy took a half step back. He stared at Andy's hand as if it were radioactive.

Andy let his hand drop and sighed. *A cold greeting in a muggy room*, he thought. He could feel sweat start to trickle down his back. As the silence stretched out, Andy looked around the room. Steel-framed bunk beds bolted to one wall. A metal desk and chair against the other wall, covered with papers. A folding chair squeezed between the bed and the desk. That was it.

There were pictures taped up all over the walls.

"You like to draw, huh?" Andy asked as he took a closer look at the curling papers stuck to the walls. "Whoa."

All the drawings were of things being destroyed. Cars, buildings, planes. Jagged lines showing the explosions arced across the pages. Pieces of metal flying, smoke billowing. Andy looked closely at a dark smudge in the corner of one of the drawings. He shuddered when he noticed tiny, jointed legs sticking out of the splotch. A bug had been squashed onto the paper.

Each of the drawings had a small signature.

Andy turned back to the boy, who managed to look both fearful and defiant at the same time. "Pyro?" he asked, raising his eyebrows.

"I like to blow stuff up. I don't care what you think," he said, not meeting Andy's eyes. He sat down at the desk. "That's how I got here. I was in a foster home. Blew up the kitchen. No big deal. I got burned." He showed his left arm to Andy. Along the underside of his forearm was an ugly, purplish patch of skin that ran from his elbow to his wrist.

"My foster parents got sick of having to call the fire department, so they decided to ship me out here."

Andy dropped his duffel on the bottom bunk and said, "Look, I really don't care what you like to draw, as long as you don't try to set *me* on fire. I have to take a leak after that kidney-pounding bus ride, so can you tell me where the head is? Otherwise, my bladder's going to be the next thing that explodes, and it won't be pretty."

Pyro gave a half grin and left the room, motioning for Andy to follow.

There were some other boys standing and talking in the hallways, some making their way to the bathroom, toothbrushes and towels in hand. A few of them glanced furtively at Pyro and Andy as they made their way down the hall. Andy caught glimpses of large black ants crawling along the ceiling panels.

At the junction of two hallways, there was a desk with a heavyset man sitting behind it. He had a graying crew cut and wore a Reclamation School, Inc. shirt. A thin younger man with messy hair, a scraggly beard, and glasses was having an animated conversation with the man at the desk. He was holding a small, transparent plastic box with something alive in it.

". . . and you're telling me you found this thing right here in the hallway?" The bearded man held the box up to the light as the thing inside scuttled around. "Geez, just look at it, there's like, six, seven, eight, *nine* legs on it. Something's going on around here, Albertson. I just found out that the headmaster sent the exterminator I brought in back home. It doesn't make sense; I mean, why bring me out here if it's not to control these bugs? And what's causing these mutations? I've been finding some stuff in other parts of the building and outside on the grounds you wouldn't even *believe* . . ." the younger man was saying.

The heavyset man held up a hand to stop the rush of words as Pyro and Andy walked past the desk.

"Well, I don't understand why Switch sent away the exterminator you called, when the things are eating us alive . . . hold it a sec, Doc. Porter . . . what are you doing out again? Didn't I just see you a few minutes ago? You've got about ten minutes before lights out. Let's get a move on." He peered at Andy and stood up. He was massive, about six foot five. "You're Greenwood, right? I'm Albertson, the proctor for this unit. Don't be a screwup, and we'll get along fine." Andy just nodded as he looked up at Albertson's neck, which was thicker than Andy's thigh. Andy noticed some raw-looking sores on the man's neck.

What is doing that to everyone? Is that from the bugs? Andy thought with a shiver.

Sensing a little tension, Pyro nudged Andy in the ribs, and they started down the hallway again.

"*Yeesh*, that guy's a moose."

"Yeah, his dad must have been an elephant that escaped from the circus," Pyro said. "I think he was in the Navy or something. As a battleship. The funny thing is that all these huge guards seem to be freakin' *petrified* of Switch."

"Who was that other guy talking to Albertson?" Andy asked as they made their way through the corridor.

"He's a freak. I heard he's some kind of scientist, a bug expert or somethin' like that. Supposedly, he's studying bugs around here. Don't know if you noticed, but we're being overrun by ants. They're getting into everything, and they sting." He held up his hand. "One of them crawled onto my hand in the middle of the night, and when I tried to shake it off, the thing stung me. They're huge, too. I've never seen ants that big.

"Anyway, some exterminators came out, but they left right after they got here. Maybe the ants scared 'em away."

Pyro led Andy to the communal bathroom, all steamed up from showers running.

Andy got rid of what felt like several gallons of pee and then brushed his teeth. Pyro waited for him outside the john. They started back to their room.

"Five minutes 'til lights out," a voice buzzed from the intercom speaker in the hallway.

Suddenly, Pyro grabbed his sleeve and pulled him into a side hall.

"Wait . . . *hey!* What is it?" Andy asked.

Pyro said in a low voice, "Just someone I don't want to run into if I don't have to." He waited for a minute, and then said, "Okay, I think the coast is clear. Let's —"

He stepped out into the main hall again, right into the large belly of a hulking kid.

"Hey, Pyro. Where ya goin' in such a hurry?" The kid grabbed Pyro by the T-shirt. He was close to six feet tall, dressed in a grubby Reclamation School, Inc. shirt, and worn jeans that were too short. A brutal nose was centered in a doughy, thick-lipped face. His head was flattened on top, which was accentuated by a buzz cut. Heavy brows shaded dark, turbulent eyes.

Pyro's voice cracked to a squeak. "H-hey, Joey . . . just gettin' back before lights out."

Joey took a tighter grip on Pyro's shirt, barely glancing at Andy.

"I been lookin' for you. When are ya going to get more of the stuff?" he growled.

Andy noticed that Joey kept glancing around at the floor, at the ceiling, as if he was *watching* for something.

"Geez, Joey, I don't know. The proctors have been changing their night routes, and —" Joey gave him a rough shake. "*Tonight!* We'll go back in tonight."

Joey sneered. "That's what I thought you were gonna say. Don't screw up, and don't get caught. I left the empties in your room."

Empties? Andy thought.

Joey let go of Pyro with a slight shove, almost knocking him over. Andy just stood there, frozen.

"Whadda *you* lookin' at?" Joey growled. He shoved Andy into a set of lockers running along the hallway and joined the teeming crowd of boys making their way back to their rooms.

"Moron," Pyro said under his breath.

"What was that all about?" Andy asked.

"Lights out in three minutes. All students return to your rooms immediately," sounded over the loudspeaker.

"Forget it. C'mon, let's get back to the room," Pyro said, leading the way back through the halls.

ANDY DREAMT THAT HE WAS IN A BLIS- tering desert, lying pinned on the ground, surrounded by little black ants. Some of the ants crawled across his face and started talking in his ear. He jerked awake. For a moment, he completely forgot where he was and turned over, but then it all came back in a rush. The whispering was coming from the room.

He sat up groggily, wiping sweat from his forehead. "What's going on?" he mumbled.

Pyro's voice came from the top bunk. "Nothing, just go back to sleep."

Something fell onto the floor with a clatter. It was a flashlight.

Pyro's voice hissed, "Fer cryin' out *loud*, Hector, you moron! What is wrong with you? You'll wake the whole place!"

A muffled voice, sounding like it came from up above the ceiling, retorted, "I'm sorry, I'm *sorry*! Don't yell at me!"

"Okay, *okay*, Hector, I'm sorry. Just keep it down, will ya?" Pyro whispered back.

Andy picked up the flashlight, and climbed a couple of rungs of the steel ladder to the upper bunk. Pyro was sitting on his bed with a pair of shorts on. Posters that had been pinned up to the ceiling were hanging loosely, pushed out of the way. One of the panels in the ceiling had been lifted aside. Another kid's head was visible through a square hole in the ceiling, just above Pyro. All Andy could see were reflections off a pair of black-rimmed glasses, which kept slipping from his nose. Big droplets of sweat dripped off his face.

"What are you doing?" Andy asked the other kid.

The kid pushed his heavy glasses back up his nose a bit, and looked at Pyro.

Pyro grabbed back the flashlight, and handed it up to the boy in the ceiling. "Stay outta this. Better if you don't know."

Andy grabbed Pyro's wrist, which was slippery with sweat. "Hang on a second. If you guys get caught, I'm in the same room and busted just like you, so I'm in."

Pyro looked at Andy twitchily, then over at Hector. Hector frowned. "It's okay by me. We can use the extra hands. You have to promise not to yell, though. There's too much yelling around this place." Andy thought that Hector looked to be on the edge of a nervous breakdown.

"I'll try to watch it," Andy replied.

"All right. Let's go, and I'll tell you about the whole master plan once we're clear of the proctors," Pyro said. "You should get rid of your T-shirt, because it's wicked hot in there."

Andy stripped off his sweat-soaked T-shirt. "Great. It's already pretty flamin' hot right here," he muttered.

"Here," Pyro said. He handed Andy an almost empty can of bug spray, with a little cartoon roach on the can, lying on its back. "There's a lot of bugs where we're going, so kill 'em when you see 'em."

Hector disappeared back into the hole in the ceiling, followed by Pyro. Andy climbed the ladder up onto the top bunk, and then into the hole in the ceiling.

It was at least ten degrees hotter in the crawl space over the ceiling. Pyro held up a finger over his lips. Andy nodded. The area they were in seemed to be a gap between the floor of the second story and the ceiling of the first. It was dark, and the heated air was stagnant, unmoving. There was enough room to make their way on hands and knees, their heads just touching the top of the space. Andy could feel drops of sweat running off him.

It was a tight fit. The boys had to squeeze between water pipes, electrical conduits, and matted pink insulation. Thick metal beams crisscrossed their path. Bundles of wires threaded around the beams, disappearing to the floors below or above. Cobwebs hung from every surface, clinging to the boys' faces and shoulders. Every few seconds, one of the boys jumped as an ant crawled over his hand. The odor of bug spray was strong in the confined space, the cans hissing as the stuff coated the bugs, the beams, and the boys.

Andy's right calf contracted painfully in a cramp as he dodged the beams. After a few twists and turns, they came to a shaft that extended downward into shadow.

Andy could feel cooler air flowing up the shaft. There was a recessed ladder that Hector grabbed onto. He started downward. Pyro followed him, and Andy followed Pyro, taking care not to lose his grip on the sweat-slick ladder. The flashlight shone on bundles of colored wires that followed the ladder downward. The black ants were using it as a highway.

As they climbed downward, feeling for the next rung in the darkness, Andy noticed that it was getting cooler. The cooler temperature was a relief. Andy was feeling parched and a little light-headed.

Finally, they reached the bottom. The ladder ended in a small space, about eight square feet. A small recessed tunnel led away from the bottom of the ladder. The wires that traveled alongside the ladder went right into the tunnel, inside plastic tubing.

"No one can hear us down here. We can take a rest for a minute," Hector said.

Andy looked down the narrow tunnel. "Where are we?"

"I found it," Pyro asserted. "I wanted to scope out this place as much as I could, right after I got here. I needed to have someplace to hide out if things got really bad." He shrugged.

"There's no way to get down here from the school. I mean, it's been blocked off, not just boarded up, or locked. Someone walled in these rooms so they couldn't be found from the inside of the school."

Andy asked, "Why would they do that? It doesn't make any sense."

"Who knows?" Pyro answered. "They forgot to do anything about the air ducts and the area over the ceiling. They must have been in some big hurry, I guess. I was lucky that I was able to loosen one of the ceiling panels in my room without the USS *Albertson* finding out. What a tool. Anyway, once I was able to get up into the ceiling, it was just a matter of trying every direction and seeing where all the passages led. I don't think anyone's actually been down here besides us for years."

He grabbed the flashlight out of Hector's hand. "C'mon, let's move it. I don't want to push our luck because Joey's afraid of bugs."

He squeezed into the tunnel and disappeared.

Hector shrugged and made his way into the small crawl space.

Andy had a moment of panic as he pictured himself

caught inside the little tunnel below tons of rock and dirt, but forced himself to follow Hector and Pyro.

They emerged in a small storage closet, after Pyro opened the aluminum grate that sealed the duct they had crawled through.

The tiny room was littered with stacks of papers and notebooks. Pyro opened the door to the closet, and ventured out.

He led them down a dusty corridor with doors lining each side. He stopped at one marked STOREROOM 3, and opened the door with a creak. Inside the large room were boxes and crates. Some of the crates near the door had been opened. Andy thought he could guess by whom.

Pyro tossed the flashlight back to Hector and climbed up to the top of a short stack of sealed plastic crates. He spread his arms and in his deepest voice (which wasn't very deep), he intoned, *"Welcome to my kingdom."* Hector giggled.

Andy asked, "What is this place?"

"We think it's from when this was some kinda army base, or defense plant, or something," Hector said.

"Yeah," Pyro chimed in, "this is where they kept stuff they didn't want anyone to find, I guess."

Hector had opened one of the bottles of water they had taken from the staff lounge and left in the hidden room, and chugged almost the whole thing down in one swig. He let out a tremendous, echoing belch. Andy and Pyro laughed.

"How long has this stuff been down here?" Andy asked.

Hector and Pyro looked at each other. "Who knows?" Hector shrugged.

Pyro went over to a pile of crates. The top one had been opened. He reached inside and took out a canister the size of an oilcan. In the light of the flashlight, Andy could see that it was painted olive drab and had numbers stenciled on it. He could make out the word INSECTICIDE RS4-B. Pyro shook it, sloshing some kind of liquid around inside. He turned to Hector and said, "There's enough left for tonight. Fill the bottles up, will ya?

"The ants started showing up a few months ago. A few of us got stung, but Switch wouldn't call in an exterminator until he got stung a few times. Turns out that Joey, who runs the biggest gang in here, is allergic to bee stings. He's petrified that he's allergic to these ants, too. I spotted this stuff the first time I came down here. It turns out that it kills the ants, so I've been filling bottles of the stuff for Joey, and in return, he doesn't have me and Hector pounded."

Hector flipped up a light switch on the wall next to the door and whined, "Awww, how come *I* have to fill the bottles . . . ?"

Pyro snapped, " 'Cause he's *my* roommate, dipstick. If he was *your* roommate, *you'd* be showing him." He grabbed Andy's arm and said, "Wait'll you see *this!*"

They left Hector filling the empty spray bottles that Joey the thug had provided, and went farther down the hall. There were papers and trash on the floor, coated with a layer of dust. A trail of footprints led to another doorway, which Pyro opened.

It was pitch-black inside.

"Hold on . . . I always have trouble finding the switch," Pyro said. Andy noticed that there was an echo.

With a *clunk*, the front lights came on. Andy gasped.

The room was much bigger than the other room, more like a warehouse, and stretched back out of view of the weak front lights.

"Wow . . . ," Andy said as he saw the immense size of the room. It was filled with barrels and crates of all shapes and sizes, and rows of boxes. Some of the barrels had words stenciled on them: ATTACK, FRIEND, FOOD, QUEEN. Other barrels bore strange symbols. He saw what looked like a big "H" with the word HEXAPOD running across it. Another was an orange circle with spiky shapes piercing it; underneath, it said DANGER: MUTAGEN.

There didn't seem to be any kind of order to any of it, as if everything had been thrown in here and then forgotten. "Whoa . . . ," Andy breathed again. He looked at Pyro, and saw a dazed expression on his face. "Hey, you okay?"

Pyro giggled crazily and ran to one of the nearby boxes, then held up what looked like a glass tube filled with some kind of greenish liquid. "Chemicals! Look at 'em all!" He raced to an opened crate, and pulled out sealed packs with warning stickers all over them.

"Hey, I don't think you should be touching that . . . ," Andy warned.

Pyro didn't hear. Even if he had, he didn't want to listen to what anyone had to say. This was his specialty. "I think whoever owned this place before the school bought it was making chemical weapons! Like nerve gas and stuff like that! Hey, let me show you the coolest thing here." He ducked behind some steel barrels and came back with a small glass vial filled with oil. There was a marble-sized chunk of silvery rock in the vial.

"Sodium!" he cackled with glee. *"Sodium!"*

Andy peered at it closely. "Isn't that just plain old salt? What's so great about that?" Andy asked. He was getting a little worried at how worked up Pyro was.

"No, it's not salt! Don't you watch YouTube?" Pyro laughed. "Sodium is a weird kind of metal. It's alka . . . alkaline, or whatever it's called. Anyways, if it gets wet, it *explodes*!" He was gesturing violently with his hands, shaking the vial.

"Take it easy, will ya?" Andy pleaded. "I don't want it to explode *now*! What are you going to do with that stuff?"

"We're gonna blow a hole in the wall and get out of here." A flame of determination flared in Pyro's eyes as they were fixed on the vial.

36

Andy realized that he had befriended the most dangerous person he had ever met.

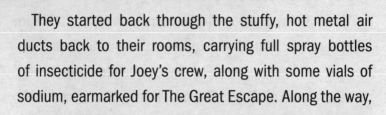

They started back through the stuffy, hot metal air ducts back to their rooms, carrying full spray bottles of insecticide for Joey's crew, along with some vials of sodium, earmarked for The Great Escape. Along the way, Andy was stung once on his right arm by an enraged ant. It felt like someone had jabbed a red-hot needle into his skin. Pyro clamped a hand over his mouth before he could scream.

Hector explained their situations as they negotiated the beams and cables in the crawl space. "Pyro is twelve, and I'm eleven. I kept getting into trouble during sixth grade, and finally a judge made my mom choose — either send me here for three months, or I'd have to go into juvie for six months. So she picks here, right? Who wouldn't? What she didn't know is that *nobody* gets out of this place when they're supposed to. I've been here for more than nine months. They keep pushing back my release. In the meetings, some lawyer for the school says that I haven't been 'rehabilitated' yet." He was getting visibly upset as he went on. "I don't know how they're doing it, but it's like they have a deal with the judge, or something. It's crooked, man."

Andy looked over at Pyro.

"Yeah, it's true, Andy. Same story with me; trouble in middle school ended in three months for me here, or a year at a worse place. But I've been here for seven months. Some of us feel like we'll never get out, so here's our ticket out of here, made of pure sodium."

Back in his room, Andy's thoughts were racing. Could Pyro and Hector be right? Could they keep him in here for longer than three months, maybe for as long as they wanted? He was twelve, like Pyro . . . maybe being older could cause an even longer stay. How could that be? Who was coming out ahead by keeping kids locked up like this? Each question seemed to raise another.

Andy's head spun with hidden passageways, exploding metals, and underground warehouses. The muggy heat was unbearable, and he stared, unseeing, into the dark, until exhaustion overwhelmed him, and he fell into a sweat-soaked, dreamless sleep.

ANDY MADE HIS WAY THROUGH THE CAV-ernous room used as a cafeteria. The clatter of plates and trays filled his ears as he negotiated the cafeteria line, dodging the bigger guys.

The large dining hall was one of the warmest and stinkiest places in the whole school. The combination of inefficient air-conditioning and the heat thrown off by hundreds of teenaged boys in one closed room combined to make one of the most uncomfortable places Andy had ever been.

And then there was the food.

The unrecognizable brown glop ladled onto his plate looked kind of gross, but Andy figured it probably wouldn't kill him. The trick was to wolf it down before the smell of whatever it was, plus the odor of hundreds of unwashed, sweating boys, became nauseating. A nice surprise was dessert: a small bowl of chocolate pudding. Andy decided he would eat that first.

He navigated his way between tables of seated boys. He could see Pyro stopped a few tables away.

Andy dodged around boys as he looked for an empty seat.

He couldn't avoid the foot some wise guy stuck out to trip him. His tray flew out of his hands, and he went down hard, catching his head against a table as he fell.

For a moment, he saw stars. As his head cleared, he realized that total silence had fallen over the lunchroom. He noticed one of the big ants crawling past his face.

"HEY!" a voice bellowed, echoing.

Andy was roughly hauled to his feet . . . face to neck with Joey, the thug who had roughed up Pyro on Andy's first day at the Reclamation School. Joey now had Andy's chocolate pudding splattered all down his shirt. The other kids at the table were all laughing and pointing at Joey. Andy felt a momentary pang of regret. He'd been looking forward to the pudding.

"I'm gonna debone your face." Joey cocked his fist back.

"Uh-oh . . . ," Andy said, and clenched his eyes shut.

A chair whooshed by Andy's head and slammed into Joey, knocking him over. Andy fell to the floor again.

Suddenly, trays, plates, and food were flying, and the cafeteria erupted in chaos.

The proctors, surprised at the uprising, belatedly began blowing whistles and pulling kids apart.

Andy thought it would be a good idea to get out while no one noticed him. He stayed on all fours, below the tables, and made his way toward an exit. School staff were streaming in, adding to the mob.

Andy reached for the door handle. *Whew,* he thought, *that was clo—*

"Goin' somewhere, twerp?" Joey growled, barring the door. He yanked Andy up by the shirt and cocked his fist back.

Andy's eyes were locked on Joey's meaty fist.

The room rocked with a loud *BOOM!* and Andy was thrown to the floor again. Chips of plaster rained down on the crowd, and everyone stopped dead.

Andy slowly stood up. Acrid smoke drifted through the

air, and he could see water jetting from a wall across the room. Someone had *blown up the water fountain*. It had been ripped to shreds by the explosion.

He could see Pyro through the smoke across the room. There was a demonic grin on his face, and a bleeding cut on his forehead.

Time to go! Andy thought, deciding to take advantage of the confusion resulting from the detonation. The door was only a step or two away.

As he turned to escape, he was pushed roughly from the doorway.

"Outta the way!" Joey growled, grabbing the door handle.

"*You two! Hold it right there!*" barked Maxwell. He clamped down on Joey's arm with one hand and roughly hauled Andy to his feet with the other.

Headmaster Switch considered the eight boys who stood in front of his desk. Pyro was on Andy's right, and Hector was next to him. They had been standing there for about fifteen minutes. Switch had been sitting at his desk, watching them, turning darker shades of purple as the minutes crawled by. Finally, he spoke.

"I'm *very* disappointed in you boys."

Andy bit down hard on his lip to keep from laughing. One of the other kids couldn't keep a snort from escaping.

The headmaster glared at the unfortunate boy.

"Mr. Maxwell, it seems that Master Rodriguez finds this whole situation amusing."

Oh, no . . . Hector. Andy cringed inwardly.

Maxwell replied, "Yes, sir," and stood behind Hector.

The headmaster rose from his desk and slowly walked around it to stand in front of Hector. "Let me spell out your current situation, Master Rodriguez, and we'll see if you continue to find it funny." He straightened the tight knot in his blood-colored tie. "The Reclamation School isn't like any school you've ever been to. It is run by a private group of investors. We don't answer to a school board. You have been abandoned by the public school system, as well as by your parents. You've made a car accident out of your life: poor choices, poor grades, poor future. So your parents and your school *gave up* on you." He put a pale hand on Hector's shoulder. "Do you really understand what that means? They have no hope for you and can't be bothered trying to help you anymore. It must be tragic for them: all the wishes they must have had for your future, gone, before their eyes. Yes, it must be a difficult thing for a parent to realize that it would have been more humane to have killed you at birth, rather than see the shambles you've made of their hopes and your own life."

Hector became more and more upset.

A realization hit Andy: Switch was clearly practiced at this. He cut through Hector's emotions as easily as a surgeon cuts through skin, muscle, and tendon.

Andy watched Switch verbally shred Hector without expression, but inside, he was shaking with anger. How could anyone be this vicious to a kid like Hector, who wouldn't hurt a fly? This latest outrage, piled on top of his foster father Chazz's brutality and his being sent here, was the final straw. He felt his face burning with rage. His vision narrowed until all he could see was Switch's sickly grin. Fists clenched, he started to step forward out of line, as Switch paused a moment to look out the window.

A big hand clamped down on his shoulder. Andy turned to look, and Maxwell gave him a quick shake of his head. *Don't do it.*

Maxwell cleared his throat, "Um, Master Switch, sir, I think . . ."

He stopped as Switch turned and wordlessly glared at the bigger proctor for several seconds with pale blue eyes like hardened glass. Maxwell, cowed, shuffled back a step.

Oh, my God, thought Andy. *Even Maxwell's petrified of this guy! How can that be?* He studied Switch. *There must be a reason,* he thought.

An ant was making its way up the wall across the room from the boys. Andy watched as it steadily climbed, turning its head this way and that as it surveyed its surroundings. Switch caught sight of it as he paced. He walked to his desk, picking up the can of insecticide. He gave it a brief shake as he strode to the wall. The ant continued its progress. It was just at Switch's eye level.

Switch leaned close, until the tip of the can was about a half inch from the unfortunate bug. He pressed on the actuator, and the bug was instantly covered by poisonous liquid. It dropped to the floor, where it twitched fitfully, its legs struggling to right itself. Switch slowly raised his foot and stamped down hard. Andy could hear the crunch of the bug as it was squashed flat. Switch turned to face the boys, a twisted smile on his face, and straightened his tie.

He continued, "My job is to straighten you out, because they couldn't. They've given me a free hand. Even the juvenile court system isn't looking at us too closely. I can hold any of you as long as I deem necessary. Do you understand that? One phone call to the judge who sent you here, and I can double or triple your stay at Reclamation.

"So, what do you think now, Master Rodriguez? Do you still find your situation humorous?"

Hector gulped and shook his head.

Switch walked back to look out the window behind his desk. The heat was rising in waves from the baking landscape.

In a mild voice, he said, "It was very . . . unusual the way that drinking fountain malfunctioned, wasn't it, Mr. Maxwell?"

"Yes, sir," Maxwell replied quickly. "Almost like it was blown up, sir."

Switch turned to face the boys again. "Yes, my thoughts exactly. But wherever would one of our students find explosives? Perhaps one of you boys can shed some light on that question?" Switch paced along the lineup of boys. He glanced at Andy, and then stopped in front of Pyro.

"Master Porter. This seems like something that would appeal to you, what with your interest in incendiaries. Do you know anything about how that drinking fountain was destroyed?"

Pyro's eyes were wide. He slowly shook his head.

The headmaster frowned. "No, no, of course not. Any of you?" He looked at each of the boys in turn. Nobody moved a muscle.

"Disappointing." Switch slowly circled his desk and sat down. He leaned forward with his elbows on his desk, fingers interlaced. He shook his head slightly. "Perhaps a few days of 'contemplation' will help you to see the light. Mr. Maxwell, take them to the meditation section."

Maxwell said, "Sir, the solitary . . . I mean *contemplation* rooms are being repainted. How 'bout we put them in Block Six? Those rooms aren't being used right now, and they all have dead bolts on the doors."

"Excellent. That will do nicely. See to it."

"Right away, sir. All right, you little hoodlums, let's move it." Maxwell opened the office door, and the boys, feeling a sense of doom settling over them, filed out.

The walk out to Block Six was short, but blistering. The boys squinted as they stepped out into the late afternoon heat.

Block Six was a small building a few hundred feet from the main complex. There were no windows to disrupt the monotony of the light gray concrete walls. Maxwell touched the door latch, and pulled back quickly, swearing. He took a handkerchief out of his pocket, draping it over the heated metal, and unlocked the latch. The heavy door swung open, and they went in.

Inside the small building, the air was sluggish and still. It was even hotter inside than it was outside.

He herded the boys into a large room, empty of furniture,

and flipped on the lights. The paint was peeling, and there was a layer of dust on the floor. It felt like no one had been in this building for months. Attached to the room was a bathroom with stained tile floors and chipped sinks and toilets. The smell of ammonia and who knows what else was strong.

"All right. Sit down and keep your mouths shut. Try to keep from killing one another for a few minutes."

Joey said sullenly, "I'm hungry."

Maxwell turned around at the door. "Shoulda thought about that before you trashed the cafeteria. You're all on bread and water for three days."

The boys groaned.

He closed the door and locked it.

The boys spread out and sat on the floor with their backs against the wall. Andy sat with Pyro and Hector. He didn't know the other boys, except one.

Joey sat across the room, staring at them. "You three are *so* dead," he spat.

"Great," Hector muttered under his breath.

A few minutes later, the door was unlocked and opened by one of the other proctors. He placed some loaves of plain bread and a few gallon containers of water on the floor just inside the doorway. "Share and share alike, ladies. You'd better finish this off, or the ants will. I'll check back on you later." He closed and locked the door behind him.

Andy could hear his footsteps leaving the building.

Joey got up, and started to make his way across the room where Andy, Hector, and Pyro were sitting.

"Joey. Don't even think about it," one of the seated boys said.

"Stay out of this, Shields. It ain't your problem," Joey said.

Andy watched as two boys stood up and approached Joey. One was only a little taller than Andy, with freckles and sandy brown hair falling in his eyes. He had broad shoulders, and carried himself as if he wasn't afraid of Joey. The other boy was taller and leaner, with large, intense eyes gazing from a dark-skinned face. His hair was clipped very short, and Andy could see drops of perspiration on his scalp.

"I'm makin' it my problem. Sit down and shut up before we get in any more trouble. Or we'll make you."

"Oh, like I'm really afraid of you, Reilly. What are you gonna do, bite my kneecaps?" Joey sneered.

"You don't have your backup now, Joey. We could wipe the floor with you," the other boy said.

For a moment, Andy thought that Joey was going to take a swing at one of them, but he walked away to the other side of the room, muttering, "Not worth stepping on roaches like you, anyway."

Reilly watched Joey cross the room, and then looked back to Andy. "Looks like you have a friend for life, there," he said with a wry grin. "I'm Reilly, and this is Shields."

"Hey, thanks for stepping in. I think he would have killed me," Andy said ruefully.

Shields nodded. "Joey's an idiot, but he's a *big* idiot."

"The two of us got here just before Joey," Reilly said. "He's been trying to take the place over. He recruited a bunch of losers even dumber than he is. We've been getting as many of the guys as we can to look out for one another. Take my advice: Don't go anywhere by yourself. Joey'll have his goon squad looking for the opportunity to pound you."

"How did you two get thrown in here?" Andy asked.

"A couple of Joey's buddies thought they'd take advantage of the food fight, and tried to gang up on Reilly,"

Shields said, with a chilly smile. "They didn't get away with it, but the proctors grabbed us, and let the goons go."

The ceiling lights flickered, then turned off and on three times.

"Lights out in fifteen minutes," Pyro said softly.

Andy and the other boys lay down on the cooling concrete. When the lights dimmed, and then died, he curled up on his side, his face scratched by the grit on the floor. *Is this what my life is going to be like?* he asked himself. *Falling from one awful situation into the next?*

Heavy thoughts settled on him like a stifling blanket. He saw his life stretching ahead like an empty road leading nowhere. He closed his eyes and slept.

Andy woke up suddenly in the middle of the night. Something had jostled him. He sat up and tried to clear his head. Pyro and Hector were a few arms' lengths away. Too far to bump him.

Suddenly, there was a loud *CRRRACK* and the floor started to shift.

The other boys were shaken awake, panicked and screaming.

The room shook violently. Andy tried to stand up, but couldn't keep on his feet. Rolling vibrations passed through the floor. Doors rattled in their frames.

Andy heard muffled crashes and bangs as fixtures and objects in other rooms were thrown about. The sound of shattered glass reached him as the windows in the main building were broken. Muffled explosions flung clods of dirt against the building.

Joey crawled to the door and began trying to open it, but it had been locked when the proctor left. He kicked it a few times with no success.

Someone shouted, "Get into the corners!"

Andy felt his way along the walls, bumping into the other boys in the darkness.

The heavy shaking continued for what felt an eternity, but in reality must have only been seconds. Alarming creaks and groans sounded from the walls and the floor. Andy was starting to feel sick from the erratic motion.

The shaking subsided to a rolling motion that continued for several seconds, with an occasional tremor rippling through.

"I think it's stopping!" Andy said. The rolling stopped,

and the room was still. The only thing moving was the dust, swirling around the frightened boys. He stood up slowly. "Is everyone okay?"

Joey retorted, "Who died and made you king?"

Reilly's voice sounded from the dark. "Joey, I swear, if you don't shut up, I'll put your face through the freakin' wall."

Pyro said, "Hey, they'll have to check on us, right? They won't just leave us out here, right?"

"I don't think we'll be the first thing on their minds after that earthquake," Hector said.

As the dust settled, the boys sat with their backs against the walls, staring dully into the darkness.

Andy was exhausted, but so full of adrenaline that he couldn't think straight. All he could do was wait for someone to let them out.

The sound of Joey hammering at the door woke Andy. "C'mon, let us out of here!" he yelled.

Light from around the door frame lit the room well enough to see. Hours had passed since the earthquake, and no one had bothered to check on them. They were all getting hungry and thirsty. They had finished off the last of the water earlier, and needed more.

Andy went to the door. Joey gave it one last kick, then moved aside.

The door frame had been twisted by the quake. He took a look at the lock. It rattled when he pushed on the door.

"Hey . . . hey, you guys! I think the lock's broken. The door is just stuck. C'mere and help me."

Pyro and Hector joined him.

"If we all hit it at once, maybe we can bust it out of the frame."

"Okay . . . one . . . two . . . *three!*"

The three boys kicked the door. Joey laughed at them.

"Again," Andy said. Another kick. The door didn't budge.

"Again."

This time they heard a splintering *crrack!* from the door. The other boys hurried over to help. A few more kicks, and the door started to give.

From across the room, Joey yelled, "Outta the way!" He ran at the door, throwing himself into it. The door splintered into two pieces, and Joey went sprawling into the short hallway outside the room.

The boys piled out. Reilly said, "Let's see what's going on around here." They started making their way to a fire exit door. The walls had large cracks running through them; ants crawled out of them, over the walls. Chips of plaster covered the floor. Dust swirled in the warm air.

Reilly pushed open the fire exit door. No alarm sounded. The heat and light pounded down on them as they left the outbuilding and walked toward the main building. A hot breeze blew past them, raising dust. "Wow, it's good to be out of that hotbox," he said. He stopped dead when he saw the damage to the school. "Whoa. Look at that."

Most of the windows in the main building had been shattered. Some of the exterior walls were damaged, with deep cracks running through the cinder blocks. It looked like part of the roof had fallen in. Smoke and dust were billowing from within.

"Geez, check this out!" Hector waved them over. There was a three- or four-inch-wide crack in the earth. The section they were standing on was several inches higher than the ground on the other side.

"Holy smokes!" said Pyro. Andy whistled.

They stepped across the crack and headed to the main building.

The first door they reached was locked. So were the second and third. They pounded on the doors and shouted, but no one responded.

"Electronic locks," Andy said. "They must have been locked when the power went."

Shields said, "That's stupid. Wouldn't they have some, I dunno, generator or something that would start up in a power cut?"

Andy shrugged. "That would make sense. Maybe something happened to it."

The closest windows were unbroken, and about eight feet off the ground.

"If we could make it up to one of those windows, maybe we could break it and get in," Andy said.

Joey sneered, "Unless you're gonna grow a couple feet, it's too freakin' high."

Andy said, "Hector, Pyro: You guys go back into that building we were held in, and see if you can find something we can use to reach that window. Maybe there are some file cabinets, or boxes, or something like that we can stack up." They nodded and hurried back to the outbuilding.

"Who's got a good throwing arm?" Andy asked, picking up a rock from the ground.

Joey grabbed the rock from Andy and flung it toward the window. The rock bounced off the wall, several feet short.

"You throw like a girl," Reilly said. He picked up a rock and threw it. It cracked the window. "Shields, you're the pitcher here."

"Yup, Major League someday," Shields said as he picked up a rock. The thin, lanky boy wound up and let it fly. The rock crashed through the window. The boys stood there, expecting someone inside the building to start screaming.

Nothing.

The fire door to the outbuilding slammed open. Pyro and Hector were dragging an empty filing cabinet between them. Hector waved and yelled, "Hey, look what we found!"

Reilly stepped close to Andy. "That's good. We have to get inside and get some water." He jogged over to help with the metal cabinet. Andy realized with a start that Reilly and the other boys were actually *listening* to him, treating him with the respect given to a leader. It felt good.

The cabinet stood within a couple of feet of the window ledge. One by one, the boys carefully climbed on top of the filing cabinet and hauled themselves through the open window. As Andy reached the top of the cabinet, he heard something. He stopped climbing for a moment.

"Anyone hear that?" he asked.

Hector, climbing in front of Andy, listened. "You mean that . . . buzzing sound?"

"Yeah. What is it?"

The sound was a chirping buzz, coming from all around.

"Whatever it is, I don't like it," Hector said. He and Andy climbed in through the window.

The main complex had lost power as well. Cracks crisscrossed the walls. The boys made their way slowly through the darkened halls of the school.

Pyro's voice quavered. "Where is everybody? What's all over the floor? What, did the toilets overflow in here?"

"Something's all over the walls, too," Shields said. He wiped his hands on his pants after Pyro's remark about the toilets.

"And what is that *smell*?" Reilly exclaimed. "It's like something *died* in here. Yikes."

"Hold on a second," Andy said. He checked in one of the offices off the corridor they were in. He could see papers scattered all over the floor. He opened the desk drawers and rooted around a bit. "Aha!" A small penlight was in a tray filled with pens and pencils. He clicked it on and panned it around the room.

"Oh, no . . ."

He stumbled back out to the hallway, shining the penlight around.

"It's . . . it's *blood*!"

Blood was smeared along the walls and spattered on the floor. It was everywhere, as if it had gushed and sprayed from the many cracks in the walls.

"Hey, this is a joke, right?" Joey said, his voice cracking. "Where is everybody? What happened here? *Where is everyone?*" Andy studied Joey for a moment. A few hours ago, he had feared the bigger boy, but now, the bully was almost paralyzed by shock, whimpering in fear.

A sharp chittering sound echoed faintly through the hall.

The boys continued searching the building. The phones were dead, electricity was off, and if there was a backup generator, it wasn't working. They had found several flashlights, but no people. The blood splattered through the halls was the only indication that anyone had been there.

There was bottled water in the cafeteria, along with food in the large refrigerators, which would only keep for a short time. The boys ransacked the food, and no one spoke for the next half hour as they ate and drank so much water that they could feel it sloshing around in their stomachs.

Andy poked around the cafeteria and found additional cases of bottled water and cans of food. They wouldn't starve for a while, anyway.

"It's hot in here," Shields said. "We better find somewhere to cool off."

Andy nodded. "You're right about that." He got to his feet and went to one of the exits to the dining hall. He absently pulled open one of the double doors as he replied to Shields. "I don't know where we can go . . ." He trailed off, brushing something from his chest that tickled. He turned to see what it was.

There was something standing outside the door.

It was some kind of creature, about chest high to Andy. It was about the size of a lion, with a triangular head. Large, glittering eyes regarded him emotionlessly. Spiky antennae were touching Andy's shirt, arm, and face.

He screamed and pushed the door shut, slamming it on one of the thing's antennae. A short piece of it fell inside the room and twitched on the floor.

From across the room, Shields said, "Geez, Greenwood, what is wrong with you?"

"*Get over here!* Help me keep the doors closed . . . Something's out there!" Andy yelled desperately.

Hector and Pyro ran over. "What? What is it?" Pyro asked as Andy held the double doors shut.

An antenna snaked under the door, touching the floor, then Andy's foot. Andy yelped and pulled his foot out of the way.

The creature rammed against the doors. Andy held them closed. The doors bulged inward as the creature hit the door again. Andy was almost knocked off his feet. "Don't just stand there — *help me*!" he barked.

Shields and Reilly ran up, holding some mops and brooms. They ran them through the door handles. Reilly pulled Andy back. The creature threw itself at the doors a few more times and then stopped.

An earsplitting buzz sounded. The boys blocked their ears. After a few seconds it ceased.

A splintering, crackling sound came through the door. Andy could see the shadow of the thing moving under the doorway. He put his palm against the wood and felt it vibrating.

"I think it's chewing through the door," Andy said, backing away. "We have to find somewhere to hide, 'cause it's gonna get through."

"Hey, I know where we can go!" Hector said.

Pyro's eyes widened. "No way. Absolutely NOT!" he said.

The trip to Pyro and Andy's room took some time. They were able to climb onto a desk and break through the ceiling panels. Using the crawl space over the ceiling, the boys carefully made their way across the complex to their rooms. They could hear things moving around the hallways. When they reached the corridor near Pyro's room, they slid a ceiling panel aside to climb down. Hector spotted something on the floor.

"Hey, what's that?" He crossed the corridor. Andy and Pyro jumped down and nervously kept watch. Hector stooped to pick up the object.

Pyro directed the flashlight beam onto the thing he held.

It was the back half of a sneaker, with ripped edges. It was stained with dried blood. Hector yelped and dropped it.

"Ronnie. This was Ronnie Simon's. See where he drew some stuff on it?" Hector said. There was what looked like a guitar and some lettering on the shoe.

"Did you know him?" Andy asked. He couldn't see Hector's expression in the dark hallway, but he noticed his slumped shoulders and his bowed head.

Hector pushed his glasses up. "Yeah. He really liked to draw. A lot of the guys took over his chores if he drew stuff on their sneakers." He shook his head. "What happened to everyone?"

There were sounds out in the hall. They could hear the buzzing of those things coming closer.

From the ceiling, Reilly said, "C'mon. We'd better keep moving." The boys on the floor climbed back over the ceiling and continued their slow trek.

After making sure the hallway was clear, Pyro dropped down to the floor. He opened the door to his room and climbed up onto the top bunk and removed the broken ceiling panel to get access to the crawl space in the ceiling. The other boys joined him in his room.

"Shut the door, and everyone follow me once we're up over the ceiling. We need to figure out what to do, without that thing getting us. Let's go," Pyro said.

He turned to the others. "Do me a favor, and don't touch *anything*."

Don't go by yourself, get one of *your grad students to go with you.* Good advice from his girlfriend that he had ignored . . . again. *She may not get to say "I told you so" this time,* Gerry Medford thought. He had protested, claiming that this might be one of the last times he could get away alone before they were married. Now, this could be one of the last things he got to do, *ever.*

He didn't think he could run much farther. Dehydration from the heat was taking its toll. There was one, maybe two of those things behind him. Gerry didn't want to find out what they would do if they caught him. He wasn't even sure what they were. As he ran, the scientist part of his brain kicked in and tried to analyze the glimpses he'd had of the things. They weren't any kind of coyote or big cat; their proportions were all wrong. They looked about the size of a lion, but were whipcord thin. And they were fast, too. If he didn't find some way to shake them, they'd be close enough to pounce in thirty seconds.

As he crested a rocky slope, he saw the group of school buildings just a quarter mile away, and a high chain-link fence about a hundred yards from him. The fence was topped by barbed wire. Like *that* would stop him.

His lungs burned. His legs were getting heavy. He was slowing down.

Something sharp poked his back. He yelped and put on a burst of speed.

He leaped halfway up the height of the fence and climbed madly. Something heavy rammed into the fence behind him, almost knocking him off. As he reached the top of the fence, he could feel the barbed wire slicing into his hands, but he made it over and jumped down to the ground.

One of the creatures was climbing up the fence, but a second was using its jaws to cut through the fence wire.

What are these things? Gerry wondered. His eyeglasses were smudged with dirt and sweat. He struggled to his feet, and began running toward the school.

Thank goodness, he thought. He could call for help from there.

He looked back at the fence. The creature that had climbed over had dropped to the ground inside the fence and was loping toward him. The other was just about done cutting a hole in the fence. He could hear that peculiar buzzing sound that they made.

The first door he reached was locked. He pounded it a few times, then went along the building looking for an alternate way in.

The next two doors were also locked.

"HEY! LET ME *IN*!" he screamed.

A voice from overhead said, "Go around! *Go around*!"

Gerry looked up and saw a figure on the roof of the building, motioning for him to go around to the other side. He started running again. Behind him, the thing was getting close. Through his smudged glasses, he could see its huge mandibles snapping as it ran toward him.

He turned a corner and saw a battered filing cabinet

set up next to a window on the side of the building. He climbed onto the cabinet, almost knocking it over.

The voice from the roof said "Close your eyes!"

Gerry stopped climbing, and shut his eyes. The thing was only a couple of steps behind him.

Something whistled past his head. *BANG!* He heard shattering glass and felt pieces of something jab into his back and arms. *BANG! BANG!*

"Okay, get inside!" the voice said.

He rapidly pulled himself in over the windowsill. He glanced back outside at the thing that had been chasing him. It was dead, apparently. He was unable to identify the creature, which was baffling. He was a biologist, and had seen bizarre creatures from all around the world, but he'd never seen *anything* like the carcass lying just outside.

Suddenly, a wave of dizziness washed over him. He leaned against the wall, and sank weakly to the floor.

Andy, Hector, and Pyro pounded down the stairs from the roof. Andy eased the door to the second floor open a crack. The hallway was clear. The three boys quietly jogged to the window that they had directed the man to use to climb in.

Finally, Andy thought, *someone who'll know what to do.*

The boys rounded a corner, and saw him lying on the floor, chest heaving. They ran over. Pyro actually knelt down and grabbed hold of Gerry's grubby sleeve. He brushed a couple of black ants off the man's shirt.

Gerry grabbed a water bottle out of Pyro's hand and drank the whole thing in one long gulp. He dropped the bottle on the ground. Suddenly, he got a crazed look in his eyes and started retching. He had slugged the water down too quickly, and his stomach was letting him know it wasn't happy. After a few seconds, the water seemed like it would stay put.

"I have to thank you guys, you saved my life. Those things were right on me. Where's Maxwell, or Albertson?" He looked around, noticing for the first time that he was surrounded by kids. "Where are the teachers?"

Shields shook his head silently. None of the others spoke.

"Oh. Well, just take me to whoever's in charge here. I have to get some help. Those things out there are dangerous," Gerry said.

"Dude, *you're* supposed to help *us*! You're Mr. Bug Man or whatever, right?" Joey cried.

Gerry looked at them, one after another. He took his smudged glasses off and tried to clean them on his filthy shirt. He put them back on and looked at the walls and floor. His mind finally realized that the dark splashes on the floor and walls illuminated dully by emergency lighting weren't decoration.

"Oh, no . . ." he breathed.

"Come on, we have to get out of here," Hector said. He and Pyro helped the man to his feet.

A buzzing sound was audible, and it was getting closer.

Pyro led Gerry and the boys to the cafeteria. Tables and chairs had been tipped over, and there were dark smears of blood on the floor and walls. Pyro grunted as he opened a heavy metal door to a staff lounge. Some of the boys fell heavily onto chairs and a battered sofa that were scattered around the room, some rested on the cool, dusty tiled floor.

It was late afternoon, and the air was still oppressive.

Pyro, Hector, and Andy handed out water bottles and

candy bars scrounged from the lounge storage closet. For a few minutes, the only sounds were the crackling of candy wrappers and water glugging its way down throats.

Gerry splashed a little water on his glasses and attempted to clean them.

He cleared his throat self-consciously. "Um . . . I have to thank you guys again for saving my life. I don't understand what those things are, or what's happened out here, but I think the first thing to do is trade information. That way, maybe we can get a handle on what we should do. I'll go first.

"My name is Gerry Medford. I'm a professor at a college out in California."

"You aren't old enough to be a professor," Joey said sullenly.

"Well, I am. I have the diploma hanging up on the wall in my office to prove it," Gerry replied.

"Gee, I feel so much safer now," Joey muttered.

Gerry continued. "I was called out here by a local exterminator company that was hired to clear out the ant problem you have. They found out that the ants were resistant to all the pesticides they tried, so they contacted the Department of Agriculture in Washington DC. They sent samples of the ants to me, after they were unable to identify the species. That's my specialty."

He gestured to a black ant crawling past him along the arm of his chair, antennae waving. "This is a new species. I've never seen them before. I decided to come out here and look into this new species, and found out that these ants are a recent mutation. There's also a high number of defective traits I've noticed in these ants; many of them have extra limbs, body segments, things like that. The incidence of these defects is way beyond what it should be. Something in this area is causing a radical increase in mutations. I was camping nearby, trying to track down the cause outside the school grounds when there was some kind of earthquake or explosion. The next thing I knew, there were these giant animals chasing me through the desert, and here I am. I was going to head home tomorrow . . . I have to start teaching a class next week."

"What do you teach at college?" Andy asked.

"Biology," Gerry said. "I've always been interested in living things. My favorites are arthropods like insects, spiders, stuff like that. I'm an entomologist.

"Enough about me," he said. "Tell me about what's really going on around here. I was told that this is a school, but it looks to me more like a jail."

The boys took turns relating their stories and theories about the racket the headmaster had working with the law enforcement and legal system.

Gerry shook his head. "Hard to believe something like that could go on. Well, whatever scam the headmaster was running here died with him."

He wiped the trickles of sweat from his forehead and gulped down some more water.

"All right." Gerry studied the boys one by one. "There are a few things we'll have to figure out in order to survive:

"We need to understand what these things are, and where they come from. That's something I can handle. I'll need one or two of you to help me bring one of them in for a little biology experiment. I think you must have killed the ones chasing me, or they would have caught me.

"Next order of business. We need to find enough food and water to survive until we can escape or we're rescued. Water's most important. We're sweating it all away in this heat.

"We also need to locate any weapons that might help to defend us against those animals. Whatever you fired at them worked really well. We need more.

"Finally, if we accomplish all those tasks, we'll still be stuck out in the desert, miles from anywhere. We need to find a way to a town. There are probably some cars in the parking lot; maybe we can locate the keys. If all else fails, my old Land Rover is still parked a day's hike from here, but I don't think we could survive the trip, with all those creatures moving around outside.

"Okay, that's everything I can think of. If anyone has any thoughts, let's get them out on the table." He looked around at the boys.

Andy spoke up. "Pyro and Hector have something you should see."

Pyro nodded. "Yeah, I guess it's time to unveil my little stash. Come on."

The boys led Gerry to Andy's room and up into the ceiling. The heat in the tight space sucked the energy out of him as he followed the boys, twisting past beams and dodging cables and cobwebs. Finally, they descended the vertical tunnel and emerged in the hidden rooms beneath the school.

Pyro led Gerry to the hidden rooms and showed him the chemicals, military-type food rations, and the large drums with the strange labels of FOOD, ALLY, ROYALTY, INTRUDER. Underneath those titles was a complicated string of letters and numbers. Gerry puzzled over them for a moment, but couldn't figure out what they might contain. He picked up some papers that had been scattered around on the floor and were covered with dust. They looked to him to be some sort of research reports. He folded and stuffed them in his pocket to look over later.

Further searching turned up a small rack of test tubes containing samples of liquid. The tubes were sealed tight, and each had a bright orange symbol and the words DANGER: MUTAGEN printed on it. "Well, that explains some of what I've observed here," he said.

Andy looked at the glass vials. "What's a mutagen?"

"It's a substance that causes genetic changes," Gerry replied. "You understand what genes are, right? They are a kind of 'biological blueprint' that contains the information for how any living organism is structured. We know that over time, tiny genetic changes occur; those changes are called mutations. Mutations, together with environmental changes that affect an organism, are what drive evolution. Over time, the little changes build up, and organisms change and develop. These changes occur over millions of years.

"There are chemicals and physical agents that can speed up the process, making genetic changes happen quickly. Radiation would be an example of a mutagen. Scientists exposed fruit flies to radiation, and saw some really big physical changes in the flies, like crumpled-up wings, too many legs, things like that. Mutagens are dangerous because they force dramatic changes that would likely be lethal to the organism. And because genetic changes can be passed on to offspring, the mutations will continue.

"That's why I have found so many ants with nine legs, and stuff like that. There must be more of these chemicals stored here somewhere, and they've leaked out into the ground. The ants burrowing around here would ingest the stuff. I can't imagine what this place was before it became a school."

Pyro and Hector showed Gerry how they put together the sodium "grenades." A small glass vial containing a chunk of sodium in oil was taped to another vial filled with water.

Hector pulled a makeshift slingshot from his back pocket. "This is what we use to fire the stuff. We took some of the bed frames apart, cut a few pieces of metal tubing with a pair of wire cutters, and bent it into shape. Reilly and Shields are the best shots."

"Wow, nice work, guys. I'm impressed." Gerry nodded approvingly. "We need to come up with an escape plan. No idea's too crazy. Once we have some ideas, we'll weed out which ones might work best. Lie low down here for a while. I need a couple of volunteers."

Andy, Pyro, and Hector raised their hands.

Gerry rubbed his hands together and asked, "You guys ever seen a dissection?"

Hector gulped.

GERRY GRABBED A DUSTY TARPAULIN
from the basement storeroom. He and the boys snuck
up to the blistering crawlway and into Pyro's room. They
eased through the hallway, back to the broken window.
Gerry looked outside. No movement. The creature the
boys had bombarded was lying a few feet from where
the cabinet had been knocked over. Gerry went out the
window, feet first. He dropped to the ground and stood
the cabinet back up so that the boys could reach it.
As the boys came down the cabinet, Gerry spread the
tarp out next to the dead creature.

The boys didn't want to touch the thing, so Gerry
moved it onto the tarp and rolled it up. Shoving it in

through the window proved difficult, until Andy clambered up the cabinet and pulled the tarp in past the broken glass in the window frame.

As they dragged the wrapped creature down the dimly lit hall, Gerry peeked in some of the doorways into darkened offices. Overturned furniture, papers scattered. Dark splashes on the walls that had to be blood. Small shapes were littered on the floor. Gerry realized that they were bones.

"Hey, let's use this office," Pyro crowed. He gestured to the nameplate on the partly open door. It read JOSEPH E. SWITCH, HEADMASTER.

They entered the room, and looked around. The computer monitor had been smashed. A single bloody handprint streaked the wall. On the floor below it were Switch's broken eyeglasses and the can of insect repellent.

Hector stood looking at the handprint, and said quietly, "What goes around, comes around."

Gerry and the three boys hauled the bulky tarp-wrapped creature up onto headmaster Switch's spotless desk.

They were all panting with exertion, and sweating. Switch's office was still and stuffy.

"I know it's hot in here, but this is the best time for this little autopsy. Those creatures will be lying low until the temperature starts to go down tonight."

After a swig of water, Gerry asked, "Any luck with tools, Hector?"

"This was all I could find down there in the lower levels." He placed a crowbar on the table along with the wire cutters.

Andy was going through the drawers in Switch's desk. "Would this work?" he asked, holding up a gold-plated letter opener.

Gerry nodded. "Yeah, that will have to do. All right, I need someone to hold the flashlight for me. Pyro, why don't you handle that?"

He unwrapped the tarp, and they viewed the creature up close.

The thing was about six feet long, with a tough, shiny covering, almost like armor. Bumps and ridges covered the armor. Spiky hairs stuck out all over, almost like cactus needles. Four jointed legs were attached under its body. The thing's body flattened out at the rear, almost like a wide tail. The tail ended in a spike-like stinger. A massive triangular head contained what looked like faceted eyes, like a fly's. A wicked set of serrated jaws arched menacingly from the front of the creature's head. Blood seeped from holes punched through the thing's armor by the boys' improvised explosives.

Gerry swore softly. "Amazing . . ." he breathed. His mind raced, looking for characteristics that would help him understand what these creatures were.

"What is this thing?" Pyro asked, studying the grotesque carcass lying on the desk. "I mean . . . it's . . . it's . . ." He shrugged helplessly. "What *is* it?"

"It looks like some kind of *bug*. A really, really *big* bug," Hector said, wide-eyed. He poked one of the thing's legs gingerly.

"Not possible," Gerry said, shaking his head as he straightened the creature out. He started murmuring to himself as he inspected the carcass. "That could be *Formicidae*, but this looks more like *Coenobitidae*, or possibly *Lithodoidae*." He flexed one of the creature's legs. "And this is more like *Scarabaeidae*, but only *four*!" He scratched his head.

"It looks like a bug to me, too," Andy ventured. "It's shiny on the outside, like a bug."

"No, no, it can't be," Gerry said. "For one thing, it's

huge. True insects can't get this large. They'd be unable to take in enough oxygen, because they don't have lungs like we do. It doesn't have the right number of legs, either. Insects have six legs. This creature has four."

"Yeah, but what about spiders?" asked Pyro.

"Spiders aren't insects," Gerry replied as he studied the creature's eye. "They're arachnids, which have eight limbs for moving around. Spiders and insects are like cousins. They are both arthropods. Here, help me flip this thing onto its back," he said.

They rolled the creature over.

"Whoa, *whoa*. Hang on a second. Check *this* out."

Gerry tilted the creature's head up a little and pointed to a tightly folded pair of spiny arms. He extended one of the arms. It reached well in front of the creature's head. "It must use these limbs to catch its prey, like a praying mantis. Then these jaws would tear its food to shreds. . . ." He glanced at the boys and stopped. Andy's eyes were wide and staring, Pyro was chewing savagely on a knuckle, and Hector looked like he was ready to throw up.

Gerry realized that he was describing the probable fate of the other boys and school staff. "Sorry, guys."

He used the letter opener to pry open the thing's jaws. They were spiky blades that scissored against each other.

"Well, Hector, you might be right. This creature does have a lot of the characteristics that insects have: three pairs of legs, a body divided into three segments, compound eyes, one pair of antennae. Wow, look at those suckers." Gerry held one of the spiky antennae up for the boys to see. "These are really important. The antennae are used to pick up chemical signals and pheromones from other insects. It's how they communicate. Amazing." He shook his head. "But the size thing is really throwing me. Insects just can't grow this large. Part of it is the breathing problem, but another challenge would be their skeleton and muscles. Mammals like us have our skeletons inside our bodies. That provides a nice, stable framework for our muscles to attach to, and allows us to move around easily.

"Insect skeletons are on the outside of their bodies. Their muscles are attached to that exoskeleton. It works really well if you're small and light, but the largest insect around now, the Goliath beetle, grows about as big as your hand. Any larger, and their muscles can't provide enough force to move their body. Plus, you need lots of oxygen to fuel those muscles. You'd need efficient respiratory and circulatory systems to take in enough oxygen and pump it around the body to power the muscles."

He wiped his forehead. "I'm not sure what this thing is. Let's open it up."

Gerry picked up the crowbar and jabbed it into the creature's body, along the center. The hard covering cracked. He worked the crowbar back and forth, splitting the body open up the middle.

Andy and Pyro grabbed one side of the creature's shell, and Gerry pulled on the other. The creature cracked open like a lobster, revealing a gooey mass of internal organs. The smell was horrible. Hector and Pyro retreated to one of the small windows in the office and tried to get some fresh air.

"Oh, my God . . ." Gerry breathed after poking around the internal structure of the creature. "I don't believe this."

"What? What is it?" Andy asked. He went around the table to stand beside Gerry.

"Look at this." Gerry tapped on something solid inside the creature. "This stuff is made of the same material as the outer shell, but it's acting like an internal skeleton. See? This hard, clear stuff is like a rib cage."

He took the letter opener and sliced into one of the thing's leg joints. He ripped it open and revealed a ball-and-socket joint made of the clear material.

"That's part of the answer: an internal skeleton. Let's see something else," Gerry muttered. He moved back to the chest cavity, and pried apart the riblike structures. "There they are." He pointed at some pinkish organs. "Lungs. With an internal skeleton and functional lungs to pull in air to fuel its organs, there's no reason to keep an arthropod from reaching this size. What is going on here? This is some kind of brand-new organism. There's absolutely nothing like this that exists on Earth."

Hector asked, "Do you see anything that would help us wipe these things out?"

"Not yet," Gerry replied. "They're going to be tough to kill, especially with the weapons we have on hand. I think our aim has to be just escaping to alert the authorities, and letting them call in the big guns."

"If only we could make ourselves invisible," Andy murmured.

The others gave him a weak grin.

Gerry straightened up with a jerk. His eyes were wide, staring into space.

"Hey, doc . . . you okay?" Pyro asked.

Gerry slapped his forehead with the hand that had been inside the creature's guts. Andy ducked to avoid the little bits of organic stuff that came flying at him.

"Of *course*! The whole thing makes sense now! Andy, you're a genius. That's exactly what we'll do . . . make ourselves invisible."

"What, and just walk out of here?" Hector asked.

Gerry nodded. "Yes, we'll just walk out of here." He snapped a bunch of pictures with his cell phone. The power level was down to one bar, and there was a NO SERVICE message on the screen. "All right, I think I've found out everything I need to from this carcass. Let's get back to the others, and I'll spell out what I know."

During the crawl back to the lower level hideout, Andy asked, "Gerry? How do you know so much about this stuff?"

"Well, I read a lot of science books and journals when I was younger. I was really into it. When I went to college,

I thought it made sense to study something I was already interested in. Now I spend most of my time teaching classes, but I still work on a couple of research projects a year."

Andy said dubiously, "That sounds like a lot of school to me."

Gerry shrugged. "It was a lot of work, but the best thing about doing what you love for a living is that it doesn't really feel like work."

"How did you know that you wanted to be a scientist?" Andy asked.

"Well, like I said, I really was into animals when I was younger. I used to read about them all the time. I loved it.

"The thing was, my parents just didn't understand my interest in science. They had other plans for me. My dad ran a carpet business, and my brothers and I were expected to get involved in the family business when we were old enough, and that included going to college and getting a business degree. But after a year in college, I was convinced that a business degree wasn't right for me. I switched over to biology, and went from there."

Andy looked at Gerry curiously. "Didn't your parents care that you didn't want to be a businessman?" Andy thought back to a time when he was very young and had wanted to become a fireman. His mother had taken him to a local fire station, and he had been able to see the massive ladder trucks. He wished he could call on his mother now.

"They were furious," Gerry said ruefully. "They couldn't believe I did it. My dad really blew a gasket. He wouldn't speak to me for years. He thought I was crazy to get involved in a field that wasn't a road to being rich. That's all he knew. He's right in that sense; nobody gets into science to get rich. But there's nothing like exploring the world we live in to see how it all works. I've traveled to the Amazon, the deserts of Africa, and lots of other places in the world. My dad never went any farther than an hour's drive from where he was born and raised. We were just two totally different people. That happens with families, sometimes."

"Is he still mad at you?" Andy asked.

"He died a few years ago, but we were able to patch things over well enough. I think he realized that I would have been miserable if I'd been a carpet salesman, just like he'd have been miserable as a biologist. It all worked out okay."

Andy was silent for the rest of the trek back to the ladder leading underground. He'd never met anyone like Gerry before, so excited about just learning things. His excitement was contagious. It made Andy want to help find out more about the deadly creatures, despite the danger they were in. Andy had never been all that interested in science before, but maybe with a teacher like Gerry, things might have been different.

They reached the ladder leading down to the lower-level sanctuary. Gerry herded them all into the "chemical room."

"All right, guys," Gerry began, "our little autopsy showed me a few things of interest. These creatures are some kind of mutated insect. They were built, or engineered, however you want to say it."

Shields blurted out, "Built!? How . . . *why?*"

"I'm not really sure." Gerry shrugged. "I suspect that this building was some kind of experimental genetic lab before it was turned into a school.

"The reason I think they have been . . . manufactured somehow is that they have precisely the kind of adaptations that would allow them to reach this huge size.

Somebody *designed* these things. And they hoped to control them, to use them somehow."

"What?" Pyro squeaked. "How could anyone possibly control those things?"

"Normal ants use chemical signals to communicate with one another. Their antennae pick up those chemical signals, which are laid down in trails. That's why you always see ants following a narrow path back and forth when they find something to eat. The ants follow the chemical trail from their nest to the food and back. The creature I examined had well-developed antennae.

"That's when I remembered these huge drums down here." He patted the drum he was leaning against. It was labeled ROYALTY. "I believe that whoever made these things planned to use chemical signals to control them, possibly in battle, and to keep from being eaten themselves. Douse yourself with the 'royalty' chemical, and these creatures will not harm you. They'll treat you like the queen bug."

"How do you know it will work?" Joey demanded.

"I don't," Gerry admitted, "but it's worth conducting a little experiment to find out."

Andy insisted on coming along with Gerry to see if the chemicals would really have any effect on the creatures. Gerry had finally agreed, inwardly glad of the company.

The sun had dipped below the horizon, and the temperatures in the school started to cool down. As they made their way over the ceiling panels, Gerry muttered, "It's still got to be about eighty-five degrees in here."

They stopped for a water break, and as they rested, sweating out the water almost as they were drinking it, Andy asked, "I don't understand how insects can pick up a chemical trail like you're saying. How does that work?"

"Humans do it all the time," Gerry replied. "We respond to smells, which are just chemicals carried through the air. That's how perfume works. Or why your mouth starts watering when you smell a burger."

Andy felt his stomach rumble hungrily at the mention of a burger.

"Ants use chemical trails as a kind of map to find food. The first ant to find a food source leaves a trail back to the nest. That trail is then followed by lots of other ants, each leaving their own chemical trail to the food, reinforcing the original trail. Their antennae can pick up the chemical trail as well as vibrations. Some ants make a sound, or *stridulation*, using parts of their bodies as a way of signaling to other ants.

"One important use for a chemical signal is to sound an alarm if an intruder enters the nest, or ants from an invading colony attack. That's what I think this chemical is." Gerry held up a small beaker of clear liquid with a rubber stopper in it. "If I'm right, we should see a definite reaction from any surrounding creatures."

"Do you think you know what these things are?" Andy asked.

Gerry said thoughtfully, "I'm not entirely sure yet, but from the autopsy, I'd say that whoever made these things started with ant DNA. Then they manipulated the heck out of it. Some of them must have escaped before the original owners of this building left and they've been living underground, feeding on the local desert wildlife until that earthquake or explosion we had. It probably damaged the nest and forced the things to go looking for a new home."

"I guess they found it," Andy said.

They finished their bottles of water and started moving again. Dust from the crawl space covered them, and Andy's nose was running. He sneezed.

Gerry started lifting ceiling panels to find a corridor in heavy use by the creatures. He had to brush several black ants from the panels to avoid getting stung. They knew they were getting close to the big bugs when that weird buzzing noise they made grew louder.

The third corridor they checked was alive with a stream of the giant creatures moving swiftly up and down the hallway. They climbed over one another, touching antennae as they passed. The buzzing was deafening.

"Jackpot," Gerry said to himself grimly. A shiver ran up his back. Despite his intense interest in the giant bugs, he was petrified about actually standing face-to-antennae with them.

He poured a small amount of the liquid onto the back of an ant passing directly below.

Andy gasped at the speed and ferocity of the other bugs as they immediately turned on the unlucky "intruder." The buzzing rose to a tortured shriek.

The creature was immobilized as the surrounding bugs clamped their serrated jaws on its legs.

Suddenly, a huge shadow fell over the unlucky bug as a massive head and mandibles came into view.

"Oh, man," Gerry breathed. This creature was built differently. Its legs were shorter, but the size of the head and jaws was huge. Tiny eyes reflected pinpoints of light as the head moved back and forth, antennae touching the ground.

"I think that's a soldier," Gerry said above the noise.

One of the soldier's spiny antennae touched the bug drenched with the "intruder" chemical. The soldier jerked as if from an electric shock. The mandibles opened wide, and snapped shut, neatly slicing the captive's body in two.

Andy felt a scream welling up inside him and clapped his hand over his mouth as it forced its way out.

The soldier's antennae quivered, and it raised its massive head toward the ceiling, where Andy and Gerry watched. The head tilted this way and that as the soldier tried to sense their presence.

Gerry clamped his hand on Andy's shoulder.

The soldier raised itself as high as it could, its jaws reaching within a couple of feet of Andy. It stood motionless for a few seconds. It seemed to know that they were there, but couldn't pinpoint their presence.

It returned its attention to the dead bug in the hallway.

The rest of the creatures waded in and started cutting the unfortunate bug into smaller pieces.

Within a minute, the attackers carried off bits of the dismembered worker, and the excitement was over. The soldier left, and regular traffic in the corridor started up once again.

Gerry slowly lowered the ceiling panel and motioned for Andy to start making their way back to the others.

"I think that stuff works," Andy said weakly.

By the time Gerry and Andy reached the coolness of the boys' underground hideout, sweat was pouring off them, making dark spatters on the dusty cement floor.

Pyro leaped to his feet, his eyes wide. "So? So? How'd it go?"

"Yeah, did that stuff work?" Reilly asked.

Andy nodded tiredly. "Yeah, it worked. It was like a feeding frenzy."

Hector looked at them. "Well, that's good, right?"

"Yeah, it's good," Gerry said, wiping his glasses on his filthy shirt, "but I think there's another problem."

A burst of hysterical laughter bubbled up from Joey's chest. "Another problem? *Another* one? You mean besides being stuck in this jail for kids in the middle of the desert? Besides the giant earthquake? Besides being chased by huge, mutant, man-eating bugs?"

"Hey, man . . . take it easy." Shields put a hand on Joey's shoulder.

Joey shook the hand off angrily. "You all think this college boy's gonna get us out of here? Those things wiped out everyone at this school but us! *This* idiot" — he gestured toward Gerry — "wants us to just *walk* right through them!" He cackled madly. *"Guess who's coming for dinner?!"*

Reilly stepped up to Joey and punched him in the face. He clenched his jaw tightly and said, "Shut up, Joey, or I'll put your head through one of these crates."

Joey had about thirty pounds on Reilly, and towered over him by a good five inches, but he backed down immediately, touching his reddening cheek, mouth trembling.

Reilly turned back to Gerry. "What kinda problem?"

Gerry said, "There seem to be different castes, or types, of bugs. The ones I had seen so far were workers. Andy and I saw one that had to be a soldier. From that observation, and what I saw in the autopsy, I think these things are based on some kind of ant. If that's true, then it's possible that they could spread from here very quickly."

"I don't get it," Pyro said. "What do you mean, 'other types'?"

Gerry replied, "Well, in a typical ant colony, you've got workers, soldiers, sentries, foragers, the queen . . . depending on the genus of ant, there could be seven or so different castes, each with a specialized body type and duties in the colony.

"I need to find out if that holds true for these gigantic bugs. I have to find out all I can before we get out of here. We have to understand them in order to deal with them."

A small rain of dust fell from the ceiling.

"Hey, does anyone else hear that sound?" Hector asked, hesitantly.

The boys fell silent. A crunching sound could be heard faintly.

Gerry said, "They're tunneling through the dirt, spreading the nest out underground. It's possible that their mandibles are strong enough to cut through the concrete foundation.

"I need to go on a little reconnaissance mission to scope out this nest. I'll soak myself with the royalty pheromone, and I should be able to walk around without being attacked.

"While I'm gone, I need you guys to map a route out of here. You all know the layout of this place better than I do."

Gerry poured out some of the royalty chemical into a small flask and sprinkled it liberally on his arms, head, and clothing. "I'll be back soon, guys. Hang tight." He left the room, and Andy heard him climbing the ladder that led to the classrooms.

The boys looked at each other silently. Their faces reflected the fear and exhaustion they'd been immersed in since the earthquake.

Andy made his way to the wall and hesitantly placed his ear against it.

The crunching sound was getting steadily louder.

7

GERRY GINGERLY PICKED UP THE CEIL-
ing panel and moved it over to the side.

The corridor was empty. He lowered himself down to the floor, dropping the last couple of feet. He looked back up at the hole in the ceiling. It was too high for him to jump. The only way back up would be to have something to stand on.

Hopefully, he'd find that while he was looking around. *Don't forget to look before you leap*, Rachel always said. She would have been right again; this was not a good idea. If anything happened to him, those boys would be on their own again.

The chemical he'd splashed on his shirt and pants had dried to a sticky consistency. Trickles of sweat, either from the heat or the state of fear he was in, plastered his grubby T-shirt to his skin. He needed a hot shower and about a month of sleep.

A shadow played across the end of the hallway, in the beams of a working emergency generator light. Something was coming around the corner.

He stood still, fighting the urge to run screaming in the other direction.

The shadow stopped for a moment. A ratcheting buzz echoed in the hall.

Gerry could hear the clattering of the thing's clawed feet as it came toward him.

It was a soldier. The thing was huge, the size of a large tiger. Its bulk took up most of the width of the corridor.

Something was different about this one, Gerry noticed. There was another bug on top of the massive head with its curved, spiky jaws. The rider was a smaller bug, about the size of a small dog. This creature had a spindly body, with sticklike legs. Large, faceted eyes studied him.

Just like the sentries in a leaf-cutter ant nest, he thought excitedly.

The sentry's head and antennae twitched quickly. It was getting ready to move.

He took a step back without thinking.

The smaller bug vaulted from its perch on the soldier's head to land on Gerry's chest, attack limbs flexed, knocking him down to the tiled floor.

He screamed and clenched his eyes shut, sure that the next thing he would feel would be his guts being sliced out of him.

Instead, the creature's antennae flicked over him, touching here and there.

Then it was gone. It had leaped back to its post on the soldier's head. The sentry and soldier touched antennae. The soldier lumbered past Gerry down the corridor.

Gerry sat up and watched the pair stalk down the hallway and disappear around a corner. He removed his glasses and wiped them on his shirt. They were still spotted with grime and sweat. He continued farther in toward the creatures' nest, his heart pounding.

Reilly and Shields were making more slingshots out of metal brackets bent into shape, with rubber tubing stretched between the "arms" of the bracket.

"Hey, Shields. Where did you learn to make a slingshot out of spare parts like this?" Reilly asked as they worked.

"My dad," replied Shields. "He's a sniper in the Marines. He spent some time in Afghanistan, and picked up some things from the locals." He grinned. "He showed me how to do a few things. I never thought it would come in handy, though."

"Wow, awesome," Reilly said. "My old man works in a chop shop. All I learned how to do is hot-wire cars."

Andy, Pyro, and Hector were making sodium grenades by filling glass tubes with a little chunk of sodium and strapping them to other small glass vials filled with water. A small ball bearing taped to the two vials would smash both on impact, mixing the water with the sodium and resulting in an explosion.

Joey was supposed to be gathering food and water for the journey once they left the school, but he sat staring at the walls until one of the other boys reminded him to get back on task.

"What's up with Joey?" Hector whispered, as Joey once again stopped packing and just sat facing away from them.

Andy shook his head. "I don't know. He's lost it, freaked out, I guess."

Pyro snorted, "He was a tough guy when he was the biggest thing around, but now, when the tables are turned, he's just a huge wuss."

"He'll be all right when we get out of here," Andy said. He frowned. "That chemical stuff Gerry is using is great and everything, but I think we need a nice big distraction to tie these bugs up while we're trying to get away. I have an idea, but I'm not sure how to make it work. That intruder chemical really made the bugs go nuts. If we could douse half of the bugs with that stuff, the other half would attack them. We'd be fine, because we'd have the royalty stuff on us. Both groups would recognize us as . . . I don't know, queen bugs, I guess. It might make it easier to get out."

"Yeah, *yeah*! That makes sense," Hector exclaimed.

Andy grimaced. "The only part I can't figure out is how to douse a bunch of the ants all at once."

"Hmmm, yeah. I don't know how we could do that." Hector frowned.

Pyro stopped taping a grenade together. He got a faraway look in his eyes.

"Pyro, you okay?" Hector asked.

Pyro looked up at the ceiling and pointed. "I think I know how we can do it."

Andy and Hector looked where he indicated. All they could see were ceiling panels, light fixtures, and some cobwebs. Hector shrugged at Andy.

"Sorry, Pyro, we don't know what you're . . . ," Andy said.

Pyro sighed, exasperated. "Look, right there! That thing sticking out from the ceiling is a sprinkler head. All the rooms and hallways should have them. *We use the sprinkler system to soak the bugs!*" Pyro crowed.

Andy laughed. "Brilliant!"

Every hair on Gerry's head felt like it was standing straight up. He couldn't remember ever having been so absolutely terrified and fascinated at the same time.

Whoever had changed . . . no, *engineered* these

creatures had done an amazing job. They had everything they needed to survive, adaptations of both insects and vertebrates. They had what looked like an ant-type social organization, which was fairly sophisticated. He could spend the rest of his life studying these things. *Of course*, he thought, *my life could be over in a matter of minutes.*

He'd been walking through the school's hallways, trying to get a sense of how this colony or nest was set up. The bugs were everywhere, scuttling back and forth. He tried not to jump in fright every time a pair of antennae touched him, checking his "taste."

Gerry was getting bone tired. He'd just finish checking this corridor and head back. Another of Rachel's favorite sayings popped into his mind: *Don't tempt fate.*

He saw a double doorway at the end of the hall. The doors had been ripped off their hinges. Young worker bugs, about the size of greyhounds, bustled in and out of the doorway. The ones going in were carrying whitish objects.

They looked like eggs.

He kept to the edge of the door frame as he eased past the busy workers. The room was huge, with high ceilings that disappeared into the darkness. Emergency lights in the corners cast a weak orange glow. He could see what must have been basketball hoops hanging from the ceiling.

This used to be a gymnasium, he thought. *Now it's a nursery.*

Large, shadowy shapes were suspended from the dark ceiling. Tiny, quick-moving bugs crawled up and down the sacklike bundles, tending to them.

Eggs were spread out all over the floor. The workers were busy rotating them, checking them, moving them to new locations, and bringing in more.

Gerry moved slowly, cautiously, edging around the eggs on the floor. His nerves were stretched tightly. The bugs touched him with their antennae as they passed. The royalty chemical was still effective.

A wet, ripping sound made him stop short. Something was happening to one of the body bag–sized sacks hanging in the room. He took out his key ring and pointed the tiny penlight at the sound.

Several of the small bugs were perched on the sack and were methodically tearing it open. There was something inside, struggling. He moved carefully closer, fearful yet fascinated.

The sack was some kind of cocoon or chrysalis. The bug inside hauled itself out and rested, hanging on to the now-empty sack.

In the beam of the penlight, Gerry could see that this newly hatching creature was shaped differently from all the other castes. Its head was small, with large compound eyes that reflected the light. The middle section of its body, the thorax, was muscular. The legs were thin and long. Gerry could just make out the first pair of limbs, tucked under its head, twitching.

Suddenly, it moved. Crumpled structures unfolded from its back. As blood was pumped through, the structures flattened and spread out, and became transparent.

Oh, God, Gerry thought. *Wings*.

His thoughts raced. There was a limit to the distance one of these bugs could cover on the ground. Sure, it might be tricky to track down the underground nests, but it wouldn't be impossible.

A winged form could potentially escape and, if these winged versions were egg-laying queens, start new nests dozens of miles away without being detected. It would take time to find them all in the barren New Mexico landscape.

Gerry realized that simply escaping to warn the authorities about these lethal creatures was not enough. They had to be stopped here and now.

He left the nursery and made his way back to the underground sanctuary.

When he arrived, sweating and thirsty, the boys were dozing. *Poor kids*, he thought. *They probably haven't gotten any decent sleep in days.*

They had been busy while he'd been gone. Several new slingshots were sitting on a crate, and there were sodium-water "grenades" packed carefully in boxes on the floor.

Several large glass jars were grouped together on the floor. They were sealed, with labels of EXPLOSIVE, DANGER!, and PYROPHORIC. Gerry thought back to his chemistry classes. An element that was pyrophoric would spontaneously ignite when exposed to air. He studied one of the jars more closely. There was a fist-sized glob of a silvery substance sitting on the bottom of the jar, which had been filled with some kind of oil. A sticker on the jar read CESIUM.

Cesium was even more reactive than sodium. *Why*

would anyone need stockpiles of such dangerous elements? Gerry wondered.

Hector wandered over, yawning. "We found that stuff inside a crate. Pyro and Andy said we might be able to use it."

Gerry nodded. "Yeah, this stuff will be useful, if we can keep from blowing ourselves up." He looked around the room. "Where are Andy and Pyro?"

Hector looked uncomfortable. "They came up with a plan to help with our escape."

"Oh, no," Gerry said. "They're wandering around the school? We have to find them. Did they at least have the sense to splash some of the royalty chemical on before they left?"

Hector shook his head. "I don't think so. . . ."

"Wake everyone up," Gerry said grimly. "Grab those slingshots and some of the sodium grenades. Those two are going to be in trouble. The bugs will be prowling."

Gerry picked up one of the jars with a chunk of cesium in it. His mind kept replaying the ferocious attack of the bug soldier on the unfortunate worker he had doused with the intruder chemical. *If Andy and Pyro run into one of those things,* he thought, *no one can help them.*

8

"YOU THINK THAT'S IT?" ANDY ASKED.

"Yeah, it has to be," Pyro replied.

They were looking out through a doorway that opened onto the roof of the school.

Andy took a cautious step outside and looked around. The sun was just setting, and a cool breeze blew over him. It felt great after the hot, stifling air inside the school. He couldn't see any bugs, large or small. He held the door for Pyro, and then saw a small block of wood just outside the doorway, along with a trash-can ashtray with many cigarette butts buried in sand. Andy used the block of wood to prop the door open, so they could get back inside.

The two boys walked cautiously across the roof. Andy could feel the heat still rising from the tarpaper covering of the roof.

There was a giant tank made of thick plastic resting on a metal framework across the roof. It was warm to the touch.

"This has to be it," Pyro said. He pointed to the sprinkler line that they had been following through the building. A short ladder led up the side of the tank. Pyro clambered up.

There was some kind of filler cap up near the top of the tank, but it was locked.

Pyro swore. "How are we gonna get that thing off?"

Andy looked around the roof. There had to be something they could use to break the lock on the cap. He ran to get the aluminum ashcan, and handed it up the ladder. Pyro hit the cap a few times, and the cap started to crack. The thick plastic of the tank made a dull *thwack* every time it was hit. Andy took over, and with a few more impacts, the cap shattered and the filler tube was open.

They each had lugged a bottle of the intruder chemical with them. They dumped it all into the reservoir tank.

Pyro grinned at Andy. "Wait'll those things get this stuff dumped on them . . ." Suddenly, he looked past Andy, eyes wide, the grin gone from his face.

"Hey, what's wrong?" Andy asked. He turned and saw that several of the large bugs had climbed onto the roof and were approaching. Most of the creatures looked like the worker type he had seen the most of, but one of the huge-jawed soldiers had accompanied them.

The boys were frozen with fear as the creatures slowly advanced.

"If they had shown up about two minutes earlier, we would have had full jars of the intruder stuff," Pyro cried. He threw the glass container at the nearest bug. It hit the thing in the head, snapping off one of its antennae. It stumbled slightly but kept coming, flexing its mandibles. The boys climbed up onto the top of the tank. The bugs were getting closer. One reached the ladder and started to climb up.

A shout came from the doorway. *"Close your eyes!"*

The creature on the ladder exploded. Andy and Pyro shielded their faces with their arms. Small slivers of glass stung as they flashed past.

More explosions flashed, blasting legs, heads, and antennae to slimy, exoskeletal bits.

The soldier was undamaged. It was still approaching single-mindedly.

Andy saw Reilly and Shields emerge from the doorway that led to the roof. They were using homemade slingshots with the sodium-and-water grenades as projectiles.

The sharp crack of the detonations and the hail of broken-glass shrapnel weren't stopping the soldier bug. Its huge jaws bit down on the ladder railing and cut through the metal. Pyro was screaming, and Andy kept pushing him farther along the top of the water tank, trying to stay out of the creature's reach. It was scrabbling with its claws at the plastic tank, but it couldn't grip the smooth surface.

Gerry pushed his way past Shields and Reilly out onto the roof. He cupped his hands around his mouth and shouted something, but Andy couldn't hear what it was because of Pyro's panicked shrieking. He grabbed Pyro and clamped a hand over his mouth.

"Get behind the tank!" Gerry was calling. He held a

glass bottle the size of a milk carton, filled with oil and some kind of silvery liquid.

The giant bug was still trying frantically but unsuccessfully to climb onto the water tank.

Andy grabbed Pyro's arm and slid off the tank. They landed clumsily on the rough tarpaper that covered the roof. They both hugged the ground, trying to make themselves as flat as they could.

They heard Gerry's grunt as he heaved the jar, and the smash of the glass as the jar hit the ground.

A thundering *BOOM* shook the roof. The sound waves hammered their ears.

Andy looked up to see the soldier bug blasted over his head in several flaming pieces, falling over the side of the building. There was a heavy *thud* as the creature hit the ground.

Reilly and Shields ran around the tank and helped Pyro and Andy get back to the doorway into the building. More bugs were climbing up exterior walls of the building and hauling themselves onto the roof, and they were ticked off. They scuttled across the roof, with mandibles snapping and abdomens held aloft, stingers at the ready.

Gerry was at the door, waving them in frantically. "C'mon, c'mon! Hurry up!"

"Geez, what was that stuff?" Andy blurted as he ducked through the doorway.

"Cesium," Gerry said, watching for any more movement out on the roof as Pyro and Shields squeezed into the narrow hall. "It explodes when it's exposed to air. Very unstable. More dangerous than sodium."

"Wow, really?" Pyro asked excitedly. "Got any left?"

Gerry pulled him in through the doorway and slammed the metal door as a couple of the smaller sentry bugs launched themselves at it. He could feel the impact through the metal as they bounced off.

The boys struggled to catch their breath after the narrow escape.

"What do you two think you were doing out there? Are you crazy? Those things were going to rip you to pieces — you're lucky we showed up!" Gerry shouted. "What could *possibly* make you think you could just take a stroll through the middle of a nest of carnivorous —"

"Wait, *wait* a minute!" Andy protested. "We came up with a good idea and figured out how to make it work." He looked at Pyro.

"We dumped a load of that intruder chemical into the building's sprinkler system, so if we start a fire in one part of the school, all the bugs in that area will get soaked with the stuff. The rest of the bugs will tear them apart," Pyro said. "All we have to do is start the fire."

Gerry stood silently for a moment, and said, "You're right . . . that *is* a good idea. I'm just glad you didn't get killed pulling it off. Let's get back down to our headquarters; we have to figure some things out."

The boys grumbled about leaving the cooler hallways to climb back into the stifling crawl space in the ceiling, but the sight of the large number of bugs moving back and forth through the hallway stopped further protests. They waded through the creatures, being touched by flicking antennae and spiky bodies. Andy and Pyro were kept between the other boys, since they were not covered with the royalty scent.

Gerry moved a chair from one of the classrooms out into the hall under the open ceiling panel. He boosted the boys up through the opening into the ceiling.

They made their way through the cramped space, dodging metal crossbeams and power cables as they went.

They emerged into the underground rooms, which were almost chilly compared to the ceiling crawl space.

Hector was almost frantic. "Where have you guys *been*?! Look, look at this!" He grabbed Gerry's shirt and dragged him to the far wall in the room. "Listen."

Gerry put his ear to the wall, and could make out the sound of the creatures grinding through the dirt and concrete. They were getting closer. He could feel a faint vibration on his cheek against the cold cement. "That's not good," he muttered to himself.

"All right, guys," he said, "we can't stay here. The bugs are cutting through the concrete, and they'll be here shortly. We have to figure out what to do." He looked around the room. "Where's Joey?"

"He's in the next room, hiding. Right after you guys left, he started talking to himself, real crazylike. I asked him if he was okay, but he just shoved me out of the way, and left. I think he's scared," Hector said.

The other boys muttered among themselves. They had all been targets of Joey in their time at the Reclamation School.

"I'll check on Joey in a couple of minutes. In the meantime, here's what we're up against," Gerry said. He

laid out his theory about what was happening with the bugs.

"I think what I stumbled on was some kind of nursery where a winged form of these creatures was emerging. These creatures are following a typical insect life cycle, but at an accelerated rate, probably due to genetic manipulation. I found a nursery where there were eggs, their first stage. There were also some grubs, like fat worms. That's the larval stage. There are cocoon-like cases glued to the walls and ceiling, where I believe the creatures become pupa, and transform. Some are emerging from those cocoons. The technical term is *eclose*. The creatures emerging could be flying soldiers, or sentries . . . or new queens. They might be getting ready to make a break from this nest to start a new colony somewhere else.

"I thought we'd have time to alert the police or the military, and it would be a straightforward task to destroy this nest, but if winged queens emerge from the cocoons I saw, they'll go *everywhere*. It will be a whole lot harder to track them all down and exterminate them. Too many places for them to hide unobserved. We can't even wipe out fire ants, and those things are tiny!" He ran a hand through his sweaty hair. "There's even a species of ant that may be joining up into supercolonies in Europe and Japan! Imagine if these gigantic ant-things did that. They'd spread all over the world. I don't know if it would even be *possible* to stop them at that point."

Desperate thoughts raced through Andy's mind: images of bug colonies in major cities . . . armies of the world fighting these bugs hand-to-hand, obliteration of the bug colonies by atomic weapons, wiping out thousands, maybe millions of people.

"Then we have to stop them *now*," Andy declared. The other boys nodded.

Gerry placed a hand on Andy's shoulder and nodded. He realized that the boys had already been through a lot. He knew that going up against the bugs might kill some or all of them. He also knew that it had to be done.

Gerry had advised the boys to rest

up for a few hours, and then they would gather the materials they needed for escape.

Andy tried hard to get some sleep, but his mind was racing. They had decided to try to escape late the next afternoon, to take advantage of the cooler temperatures as the sun set.

The other boys were asleep, exhausted by the panic and danger of the last several days.

Andy sat up in the cool, humid darkness, trying not to wake the others. He could hear the muted digging of the bugs behind the walls. It sounded like they were approaching from different directions, getting closer by the minute. He heard a noise from across the room and saw a faint light.

Carefully making his way across the room, he saw that Gerry was awake, writing in a small notebook and looking at some dusty papers. The light was coming from his cell phone, which was dimming rapidly as it ran out of power.

He looked up as Andy approached. "Hey, you should be asleep."

"Can't." Andy shook his head. "What are you looking at?"

Gerry tilted the notebook so Andy could see it. "It's notes and drawings about these giant ants. My phone is almost out of power. My penlight ran out a few minutes ago. I wanted to take a closer look at these papers I picked up in the underground level." He spread them out so Andy could see them. "Look here," he said, pointing to the bottom right corner of several of the papers.

Squinting, Andy could make out the words *Hexapod Group*. He looked back at Gerry. "Do you know what it means?"

Gerry shook his head. "No, I'm not sure, but it might lead to whoever made these things."

Andy flipped through some of the notebook's pages. "Do you think we're going to get out of here alive?" he asked.

"Yeah. Yeah, I do. That plan you guys figured out was brilliant. You may have just saved all our lives. That was good thinking. You'd make a great scientist, you know." Gerry grinned.

Andy ducked his head, trying to hide a smile, and looked at the notebook again. "Really?" he asked. He turned that thought over in his mind. *Me? A scientist?* He liked the sound of that.

"All we need to do tomorrow is put a couple of things in place, like getting some supplies together, figuring out a vehicle to get us from here to my truck, and from there we're fine." He turned serious. "One thing I want to do is see if we can destroy this nest, or at least slow them down from spreading. If we can damage this building enough, that, along with the bugs tearing each other apart, should give us time to get some firepower here to deal with them." He yawned. "I gotta get some sleep . . . try to at least rest, Andy. Once we start moving, we can't stop until we're clear of these things."

"Okay," Andy replied. He lay down on the cool cement

with his wadded-up shirt as a pillow. It was sticky with sweat and the royalty chemical, which had an unpleasant sickly-sweet scent. He was sure he wouldn't be able to sleep.

The next thing he knew, Reilly was rousing him. "C'mon, man. It's Extermination Day."

Gerry gathered them together at one of the crates stacked against a wall. After only three hours of sleep, the boys were slack-jawed with fatigue. Joey had gathered enough water and candy bars to last a few days, if they were careful.

The muted crunching sound as the bugs ground through the concrete continued to grow louder.

Pyro blinked blearily. "So how are we getting out of here?"

"We need to get moving on a few things first," Gerry said. "We need some kind of transportation. There are cars out in the parking lot, but no keys to get into them."

Shields said, "Hey . . . what about that old bus they used to bring us all here? We can check the security office for the keys."

"Who needs keys?" Reilly snorted. "I bet I can hot-wire that piece of junk in about five seconds."

"I don't think I want to know anything more about that. Transportation: check," Gerry said. "Next, we have to set the sprinkler system off to get the bugs fighting one another." He pointed to the emergency lights in the corners of the room. "Those lights are running off some kind of generator, which has to run on gasoline or some kind of fuel. We need to find the tanks holding the fuel. We also need some way to light it. We'll check the desks in all the offices nearby. Maybe we'll find some matches."

"I want in on that!" Pyro blurted, his arm held up high.

Gerry grinned wryly. "Against my better judgment, okay, Pyro. The next thing we need to do is blow a few holes in this place. The bugs who aren't fighting will start on repairs. They won't even notice us leaving."

Andy had been half listening, trying to stay awake. He was trying to focus on what Gerry was saying, but his mind kept wandering. His eyes drifted to the wall behind Gerry. Some dust was falling down the wall in a thin stream. He regarded it quizzically.

Suddenly, a crack appeared in the wall. Andy's eyes widened. He stood and pointed at the wall, and was about to cry out when the wall split into large chunks of concrete that fell heavily on Gerry. He went down without a sound.

A bug appeared in the hole in the wall. It looked around at the speechless, gaping boys for a moment, and then drew one of its hind legs along its abdomen to signal other bugs. A loud, ratcheting buzz blasted through the room.

The boys were frozen in shock and fear. The noise stopped. The bug tried to step over the broken chunks of cement in the opening of the wall.

With a jolt, Andy recovered himself. He looked around wildly and grabbed a glass jar full of a sludgy liquid. He threw it as hard as he could. The jar hit the ant in the head, cracking its thin exoskeleton and breaking off an antenna.

The ant stopped for a moment and shook its head. It flexed its mandibles, picking up a cinder block and crushing it into pieces.

Reilly screamed, *"Kill that freakin' thing!"*

Shields grabbed a handful of the homemade sodium grenades and started whipping them at the ant. Each one detonated with a sharp *crack*, spraying glass fragments through the room.

Pyro and Hector helped, using their slingshots. The sodium vials made a humming noise as they cut through the air. The creature was covered with scorch marks from the blasts, and glass shards stuck out from it like pins in a pincushion.

Joey was screaming, standing with his back against the far wall.

The creature stopped again, opening its mandibles wide. It produced a series of short, ratcheting chirps by rubbing a hind leg against its abdomen. The noise was almost at the edge of hearing.

Reilly darted in, picked up a big chunk of cement, and caved in the bug's head. The noise stopped.

"C'mon, help me," Andy said to Hector and Pyro. They pulled Gerry out from the rubble of the wall.

"Is he . . . is he dead?" Hector asked, fearfully.

Andy reached down and felt for a pulse at Gerry's neck. "No. I can feel a heartbeat." He checked the back of Gerry's head. "Big bump back here." He saw blood on his fingers when he drew his hand back. "We have to get him to a hospital."

"Hospital? *Hospital!*" Joey shrieked. "We can't lug him around and still get outta here! Just *leave* him!"

"No!" Andy shouted. "We don't leave anybody, Joey . . . not even you!"

Joey roared incoherently. He kicked out savagely at a box on the floor. "You're *dead*!" he spat and stalked toward Andy, who stood frozen in surprise.

"That's it. I've had it with you," Reilly grated. As Joey reached for Andy, Reilly grabbed Joey's hand. He cocked his fist back, ready to throw a punch. Joey brought his other hand up to strike out at Reilly, but suddenly, it was caught from behind him by Shields. Pyro, Andy, and Hector waded in and pushed Joey back against a crate, where he was pinned.

"Five against one? Is that how you creeps fight?" Joey said, uncertainly. He had never found himself in a situation like this before. He was usually the one doing the pushing around.

"Why not?" Shields laughed mirthlessly. "That's how you operate, isn't it? It's a little different when you're the one who's outnumbered."

"No fun being on the other end of it, huh, Joey?" said Pyro.

"Hey, guys! I know what we can do with him! Let's tie

him up and leave him for the bugs. Gerry's out cold, and we can say whatever we want," Reilly said.

Hector looked nervously at Reilly, who winked at him.

"C'mon, you guys. You know I'm allergic to stings! I gotta get out of here!" Joey declared, sweating.

"Hold it, guys," Pyro said. "Maybe we can work out a little deal. Even though nothing would make me happier than to leave Joey here, we need him to help get Gerry out."

"Hey, yeah! You guys need me! I can help!" Joey said, desperately.

Reilly pretended to think about it. "Hmmm. I don't know. You're sure that's what you all want to do?"

The boys nodded.

Reilly grabbed Joey by the shirtfront, which looked ridiculous, since Joey towered over Reilly.

"All right. You're coming with us because we can use your help. I want you to remember this the next time you feel like picking on a smaller kid. When we had the chance for payback, we didn't take it." He pushed Joey away roughly.

A faint chirping whine reached their ears.

"Guys, I think we need to move," Shields said nervously.

"Unless anyone has a better idea, I think we should use the plan Gerry talked about," Andy said. "We need to get the bus running and set off the sprinkler system. If we happen to think of a way to blow the building up without killing ourselves, that'd be good, too. The first thing is to find a way to move Gerry."

Pyro pointed behind some crates. "Hey, I think I just solved a couple of our problems!" he said. "Check this out." He ran over and pulled a two-wheeled dolly out behind him. "We can use this to move Gerry around, see? If one guy is on each handle, and one more makes sure he doesn't fall off . . ."

"Yeah, that should work," Andy said.

"And this is the best part . . . c'mere," Pyro said excitedly, dragging Andy by one arm. He stopped at one of the large drums of the intruder chemical. "Help me turn this a little."

Andy helped to turn the drum around a bit. Pyro pointed to a sticker on the side of the drum. He wiped some of the dust off it.

Andy peered at it. It was a diamond-shaped label, with a symbol for "fire" on it. Underneath, it read FLAMMABLE.

Pyro broke into gleeful laughter. "We can blow up the whole building *and* all the bugs with this stuff."

"Now all we need is a way to light it," Andy mused.

Shields came up behind them. "There are probably some road flares on the bus . . . you know, for emergencies or something."

"Some of the barrels are roped together. Maybe we could use the rope to help get Gerry out of here," Hector said.

Andy nodded. "Good idea, Hector." He grabbed a cardboard carton filled with some kind of disinfectant wipes and dumped them out. "Everybody take a box and fill it with the sodium grenades, and try to take a couple of jars of the bigger chunks, too. We'll need them."

Once everyone had some of the dangerous metal, they filed out of the room, half dragging, half carrying Gerry along.

"Hey, hold it a second," Hector said. He ran over to one of the drums containing the pheromone and unscrewed the cap. He tried to give it a shove, but it was much too heavy for him to budge.

"Yeah, that's a good idea," Reilly said, and helped Hector to tip two of the barrels over. They thunked heavily to the ground, and the chemicals sloshed out, spreading all over the floor.

"YES!" Pyro crowed, as they all doused themselves with the sticky-sweet royalty chemical. "This is gonna be so freakin' *great!*"

Reilly looked down through the opening in the ceiling to the hallway below. There was sporadic bug traffic. They moved in fits and starts, touching the floor and walls every few steps with their segmented antennae.

It was hot in the cramped space over the ceiling. The sweat was causing the pheromone to run down his arms, making his hands glossy and sticky. He looked at Shields and took a deep breath. "I hope this stuff works."

He lowered himself as far as he could, hanging by his hands a few feet above the floor. A worker bug was striding along the hallway and stopped just under Reilly's feet. "Holy . . . !" he exclaimed. His hands were losing their grip. Shields grabbed his wrists.

A small sentry bug scuttled down the corridor and climbed onto the larger bug's back. They touched antennae briefly. Then the sentry reached up and touched Reilly's sneakers. For a moment, it seemed startled. Its jaws opened uncertainly, then closed. The antennae touched him again.

Reilly held his breath. He was losing his grip, and he could feel his wrists slipping through Shields's hands.

"Pull me back up!" he hissed.

"I can't hold on!" Shields grated.

Reilly looked up. Shields's face was dripping sweat, the tendons in his neck standing out like cables.

"You're slipping!" Shields cried.

Reilly felt his fingers sliding from Shields's hands. It almost felt like it was happening in slow motion. Suddenly, he slipped free, and the sound of his own scream filled his ears.

He landed heavily on the floor, cracking the back of his head on the concrete in the middle of the corridor full of bugs. He held his breath and shut his eyes, expecting to be ripped to shreds by the creatures.

"Hey . . . hey, Reilly," Shields said softly from up in the ceiling. "I guess that chemical stuff does work, huh?"

Reilly gingerly sat up and opened his eyes. The bugs

were striding around him, brushing him with their antennae as they passed. He rubbed the back of his head.

He stood slowly, shaking his head to clear it. "C'mon,"
he said, "hand that sodium stuff down, and let's get to
the bus."

"WHAT IS WRONG WITH YOU TWO? PULL, will ya? I want to get out of here, and I can't if this guy is blocking the tunnel. PULL!" Joey bellowed in the narrow tunnel.

Hector wailed, "He weighs a ton and a half."

"Yeah," Pyro agreed, pushing sweat-soaked hair out of his eyes, "he makes up about six of us. You shoulda been up here pulling, and we should have been back there pushing, Einstein."

"If I have to crawl over this guy, I'm gonna rip off your arm and beat you with it," Joey growled. "I want out of this stinkin' tunnel."

Hector groaned. Andy looked behind him and saw that the tunnel mouth was only a few feet away.

"We're almost there," he muttered. He grabbed a handful of Gerry's soaked shirt. "Then we have to get him up the freakin' ladder."

Hector swore under his breath.

Andy tied one end of a length of rope around Joey's waist and looped the other end under Gerry's arms. Joey went up the ladder first, dragging the still unconscious scientist after him. Andy followed, pushing from underneath Gerry's legs. It was slow going, but they were able to make it to the top of the ladder. They lifted Gerry onto the dolly and rolled him down the corridor.

"All clear," Andy said softly. He edged around the corner and beckoned to Joey, Pyro, and Hector, who were trundling the unconscious Gerry, slumped over a two-wheeled dolly. They were shaking with fatigue.

A few worker bugs slunk up and down the corridors, intent on some task. Each of the creatures touched antennae as they passed each other, Andy noticed. *Like they're talking*, he thought. The bugs were touching him as they strode by, stopping just for a moment. He was almost to the broken window where they had entered the school after the earthquake.

"Andy. Hey, Andy!" Hector's voice came from back up the hallway. There was a loud metallic noise. He turned back to see what the problem was.

Hector and Pyro were trying to hold Gerry up by themselves. The dolly was lying on the ground, and Joey was flat against the wall, eyes clenched shut, muttering softly. He jumped slightly as the bugs trooped up and down the corridor.

Andy rushed over to help lower Gerry to the tiled floor. Pyro was turning purple with the effort.

"Watch his head!" Hector cried as the injured scientist's skull cracked against the floor. He groaned softly, and his eyelids fluttered.

"He's not gonna be a scientist after that," Hector mumbled.

"This must be some kind of bug superhighway or something," Shields said, as he and Reilly slowly made their way through the administration offices for the school.

The bugs filled the corridors; sometimes climbing over one another to continue whatever errand they were on.

The antennae of the bugs that passed them constantly grazed the boys. So far, the royalty chemical seemed to be working effectively.

The sentries had set up "roadblocks" at different corridor intersections, perched on the heads of the massive soldier bugs. At each roadblock, a huge soldier bug would raise its head and open its jaws menacingly, halting the boys' progress momentarily. The tiny eyes of the soldiers were almost useless. The little sentries were almost like "guide dogs" for the much larger soldiers.

The sentries were more thorough with their examination, touching them in several places and studying the boys with their glittering, faceted eyes.

At the first roadblock, Reilly said nervously, "I think these little guys must be smarter than the big ones. They can tell that something's not right with us." Shields nodded.

Once a sentry was convinced by the royalty pheromone that they were not a danger to the colony, they were allowed to proceed.

The hallway that led to the administration offices was deserted. The floor was strewn with broken glass and splinters of wood. Doors had been torn from their hinges. The floor was covered with dark red stains.

"Is that what I think it is?" Shields asked. He brought a hand up to his mouth.

Reilly replied, "If you're thinking it's blood, then yeah, it's what you think it is." He looked at a dark red hand-print on the wall. "They've been through here already. There's no more . . . food . . . so they're just ignoring it, I guess."

The offices were all open, and the boys slowly made their way from office to office, gingerly crunching over broken glass, looking for anything that might be helpful.

"Hey, check it out," Reilly said. The next office they explored was labeled SECURITY. "Might be something in here."

Light from the windows didn't penetrate into the small security office. Shields whacked his shin against an overturned chair, and he swore in surprise and pain.

"Hey, a desk," Reilly said. He felt around the jumble of papers and folders strewn haphazardly across its surface. "Huh. Nothing useful on top. Let's see if there's anything in the drawers," he muttered. "Oh, yeah. Here we go," he said, and a flashlight beam lit the whole room interior. Papers and trash were strewn everywhere. Two dented steel filing cabinets stood against one wall. The drawers were stuck closed. There was another flashlight on the floor, but it had been left on, and the batteries were dead. Dried blood was smeared on the lens.

"Ugh." Shields gagged and dropped it, and it clattered to the ground. He stood with his hands on his knees, head bowed down. He retched convulsively a couple times, but calmed down. He straightened up, his eyes hollow looking in the flashlight's beam.

"What's this?" he asked, picking up a short, chunky device from the floor. He pressed a button on the gadget's handle, and a blue-white arc of electricity buzzed and crackled between terminals on the thing's end. He yelped in surprise.

"Nice find! Gimme that thing," Reilly demanded. He held it in the beam of the flashlight. "This is a Taser. We might be able to use it against the bugs. Or I might just use it on Joey."

A metal shelf was bolted to the wall, containing some

walkie-talkies. Next to them was a locked rack holding a shotgun.

Shields took the dead flashlight and banged on the tiny lock securing the gun. It broke easily, and he hefted the gun.

"Know how to use that?" Reilly asked.

Shields nodded. He broke the gun open and inspected it, snapping it shut expertly. "My dad showed me how to use a shotgun. I've been using guns for a long time. Look for a box of shells, and we'll be in business."

A small box beside the banged-up filing cabinets had been smashed open by some cinder blocks loosened by the earthquake. They couldn't find any shotgun shells, but did come across several small cans of pepper spray, which they decided to leave, since they didn't know if it would affect the bugs.

"Oh, man!" crowed Shields. "Jackpot. Check this out!" He held up a large ring of keys and a small disposable lighter. "Pyro's going to be in heaven."

They used an office chair to smash one of the glass windows that led to the outside of the school. Their shadows were long, and the breeze was getting cooler.

"That feels great," Shields said.

"Yeah, but the bugs will be coming outside soon. I wonder if it would have been smarter to wait until the morning to try to get clear," Reilly replied.

The bus was sitting in a small parking area off the main entrance to the school. The door was open. Reilly and Shields slowly crossed the dead, scrubby grass to the bus. They climbed in, and Reilly dropped into the driver's seat, trying the keys. None fit.

"I was hoping one of these would work," Reilly muttered. He ducked down to the floor of the bus and looked around the underside of the steering column. "Here we go. . . ." he said, yanking a couple of wires loose from under the dashboard. He twisted the exposed ends of the wires together, and the engine sputtered to life.

"Can you drive this thing?" Shields asked.

" 'Course I can." He pushed in the clutch, and tried the long gearshift. A loud grinding sound came from under the floor. "Oops." Reilly grinned sheepishly. He studied the gear diagram on the shift, and tried again. This time, the bus went into gear smoothly. They backed out of the parking space fitfully, and drove up onto the dirt schoolyard until they came to the broken window with the filing cabinet still standing outside.

Andy leaned close to Joey, and said softly, "Joey . . . come on. Time to go." Joey shook his head, eyes clenched shut.

Andy tapped his shoulder, and Joey jumped, pulling away. "Don't touch me!" he bellowed. He opened his eyes wide as bugs trooped by them.

A horn honked outside the window: The bus had arrived.

Hector and Pyro hefted the ladder lying on the floor and lowered it out the broken window. A hot breeze gusted through erratically. Andy looked outside. The sun was getting lower in the sky. They had to leave before nightfall, when all the bugs would start foraging for food.

Shields climbed on top of the cabinet, and poked his head in the window. "C'mon, you guys, let's move." He climbed in and helped to maneuver Gerry to the window.

The hallway was getting crowded with the boys trying to move Gerry outside to the bus. They finally lowered him clumsily outside, feet first. Reilly was waiting impatiently on the ground. The boys carried the unconscious biologist into a seat on the bus, where he slumped down against the window.

The boys were all dripping sweat and panting. The bus's engine rumbled fitfully, coughing out a cloud of gray exhaust.

"All right, everyone on board. We're getting out of here," Reilly said. "Where are Andy and that slab of meat?"

"Still inside," Hector replied, "Something's up with Joey. He won't move."

"I'll get him to move," Reilly growled, and climbed in through the window. He crossed into the hallway through the broken window and jogged over to Andy and Joey. The bully looked like he was trying to squeeze himself against the wall as tightly as he could. His eyes were wide and staring.

"What's with him?" Reilly demanded.

"Dunno," Andy murmured, shaking his head. Two bugs trooped past them down the corridor, briefly touching the boys with their antennae. "He's freaked, I guess. I can't get him to move."

"Oh, come *on*! We're almost out of here," Reilly muttered. He shook Joey's shoulder roughly. "Hey . . . hey! Get up, you idiot, the bus is right outside. We have to light this place up before the bugs get out."

Joey just shook his head, eyes clenched shut.

"We don't have time for this," Reilly growled. He took one of the homemade slingshots from his back pocket and fitted a small glass tube holding a chip of sodium, and stretched the band back. He held the slingshot a few inches from Joey's face. "Get up. Get up, you useless piece of trash, or you're gonna have a face full of exploding glass."

Joey flinched and whimpered, but didn't get up. Andy placed a hand on Reilly's shoulder, and shook his head. "Fine. Stay here, you jerk," Reilly hissed. He shoved Joey to the floor and ducked back out the window. He looked back and said, "We're leaving with or without him in five minutes." He lowered himself down to the filing cabinet and then to the ground.

"I can get him to move," Pyro said quietly from the window. He climbed into the room, dodging a bug as he crossed the corridor. He was carrying a cheap disposable lighter that he had found in the office, and a newspaper that the driver must have been reading.

He handed the fire-starting materials to Andy, and knelt down next to Joey. He put his mouth next to Joey's ear.

"Joey. Joey, come on. We have to leave now."

Joey blinked. He slowly turned his head and looked at Pyro.

"All we have to do is go across the hall and out the window. The bus is right there, and then we can leave." Pyro kept up a steady stream of calm, quiet words as the bugs marched up and down the hall.

Andy and Pyro slowly coaxed Joey to stand up.

Pyro kept up his reassuring chatter. "We're almost there, Joey, you're doing great . . . just a little farther, and we can leave."

A bug marched past, its antenna brushing Joey's leg. Joey tried to bolt, but Andy and Pyro hung on tightly.

There was a momentary gap in the bug traffic in the hallway. The boys pulled on Joey's shirt.

"Here we go, Joey. Here-we-go, here-we-go, here-we-go," Pyro said in a reassuring voice, slowly guiding Joey toward the window.

Joey clapped his hands over his face. "I can't, I c-c-can't . . ." he stammered. He shivered as a bug passed them, clacking down the hall.

"Look, Joey," Pyro said in an encouraging voice. "We're here, we're at the window." He stepped out of the window frame, down onto the filing cabinet. "All you gotta do is come outside the window. See? There aren't any bugs out here, Joey."

A cool breeze blew in through the window. Joey took his hands away from his face and squeezed out of the window, just as another bug made its way down the hallway.

Joey clambered down onto the filing cabinet, and then to the ground.

Andy sighed in relief. Shields said, "Wow. The little dude did it."

The boys could hear Reilly's voice commanding Joey to get on the bus.

Pyro's head poked back in through the window with a grin. His eyes were flashing.

"All right, you guys . . . let's barbecue some bugs!"

"WHATEVER YOU DO, DON'T DROP IT!"
Andy said as he reached down from over the corridor ceiling and gingerly lowered a quart-sized glass jar that had a liquid, silver, syrupy substance suspended in oil.

"Okay, I get it, I get it," Pyro replied testily. He climbed down from the chair and placed the jar against the wall. Bugs were moving busily up and down the hall, and the boys didn't want the jar knocked about.

He climbed back onto the chair. "I'm the one who knows about this stuff, remember? You guys wouldn't have known that cesium explodes in the air until it blew your head off," he grumbled as Andy lowered a second jar.

"Will you cut it out?" Hector pleaded. He was petrified by being back inside the school when escape was so close.

"Hector, I promise: We'll be out of here in no time." Andy patted his shoulder, and lowered himself into the waiting chair. "Just be ready to pull us up."

Pyro's eyes were like sparklers going off; he couldn't wait to set this place on fire.

They each carried one of the jars of cesium. Andy also had some emergency road flares, and Pyro had the cheap lighter in his pocket.

The bug nursery was in a large room at the end of a corridor. The windows had been covered with some kind of mudlike substance. There were many bulky cocoons hanging from the ceiling. It was dark, still, and stiflingly hot.

"Check it out." Pyro pointed to spots on the ceiling, in between the hanging cocoons. The stubby shapes of sprinkler heads projected from the ceiling. Andy nodded. They could set the fire right under the cocoons.

In an adjoining office, the boys located a small wooden table damaged in the earthquake; one of its legs had been snapped off, and it wouldn't stand on its own. Pyro found the broken leg, and they moved the table into the nursery, dodging the bugs that were striding in and out of the area, constantly checking on the hanging cocoons. Andy peered closely at one, and could see an indistinct form wrapped inside. As he watched, the thing inside moved slightly.

Pyro brought in a metal wastebasket, which he had filled with some of the papers strewn all over the floor. Andy held the table steady as Pyro placed the broken leg into the wastebasket. He was able to set the end of the leg against the tabletop. He slowly moved his hands away; the table remained standing. Andy gently let go and backed away from the table.

"Like building a card house." Pyro grinned. They placed the two jars filled with the liquid cesium on the table, letting go slowly, slowly.

A bug bumped into Andy, and he nearly hit the table. Pyro's eyes flew open wide, and he gasped. Andy managed to avoid nudging the table, and they both let out sighs of relief. Pyro tried to wipe the sweat from his eyes, but his arms were filmed with sweat as well.

Lighter in hand, Pyro gathered up a handful of papers and lit the edge of one sheet. "We're not going to need the flares; this will work. Okay, get back up to the ceiling."

Andy left; he ran back out to the hallway and hopped up onto the chair. Hector took his hand and helped him back up into the ceiling.

Pyro watched the fire eat the papers in his hand. The flames were mesmerizing as they danced across the crumpled stationery.

"Hey! C'mon!" Andy's voice from the hallway reached Pyro, and he dropped the burning papers into the wastebasket. They flared up immediately.

Pyro ran back into the hall and vaulted up onto the chair. Both Andy and Hector caught his arms and hauled him up. They watched as the fire and smoke spread.

Inside the nursery, the papers were flaring up. The metal wastebasket kept the flames contained. The table leg started to smolder and smoke started to rise.

The cocoons glued to the ceiling started to move and bulge. First one, and then more cocoons started to split open with a wet, ripping sound. The creatures inside would be free very soon.

As the table leg caught fire, the small table itself started to wobble; the two jars clinked together.

The smoke filling the room reached the smoke detectors in the ceiling and set them off in high-pitched shrieks.

The sprinklers started spraying water in a gush. Sprinklers in offices and corridors nearby also went off, trying to contain a fire from spreading. What they did was spray a large number of bugs with the intruder chemical.

The workers started scurrying about, attempting to move any undamaged eggs and immature bugs away from the fire.

Suddenly, a worker dropped the egg it had been carrying in its mandibles. It turned and bit the leg off a worker beside it.

Three workers fell on one another, ripping limbs and antennae from each other.

A massive soldier dragged itself into the nursery, with several small sentinels cracking through its thorax with their razor-sharp mandibles, and one clamped firmly onto a hind limb. Its antenna touched a worker. The soldier opened its attack mandibles wide and sliced the worker's head off, seconds before the fire consumed it.

The bugs became frantic as the fire and smoke spread, and more sprinklers went off. The chemical added to the water drove them crazy. They attacked one another: soldiers, sentries, and workers.

Some chemical signal reached the bugs in the cocoons, and they ripped out of their enclosures, the newly eclosed princesses crawling across the ceiling to escape.

After seeing the bugs go into a wild frenzy, attacking and killing one another, Andy said, "Okay, guys, let's get outta here." The three boys moved as quickly as they could through the maze of wires and girders above the ceiling to where they could escape from the school.

The sprinklers finally slowed, then stopped as the tank mounted on the roof of the building finally ran dry. Fumes from the intruder chemical sprayed out from the sprinklers had spread throughout the entire building, driving the creatures into a killing frenzy. Severed legs and antennae were everywhere.

The smoke and flames were spreading and growing thicker. The bugs didn't seem to notice. They were all locked in combat with one another. One of the enraged creatures crashed into the damaged table holding the two jars of cesium. The broken leg was jostled, and it fell. The table tipped, spilling the two jars, which smashed to the floor.

The cesium splashed free of the oil, mixing with the air and water as spatters of the golden liquid metal were hurled around the room.

The cesium reacted powerfully, exploding like a bomb. Blindingly bright purple sparks flashed, and roiling clouds of hissing smoke rolled through the room. Chunks of cement, splinters of burning wood, shards of glass, and bug parts were blown through the halls. All the windows in that wing of the school shattered.

A hot blast of air pushed through the crawl space, as the volatile chemical detonated. The boys grabbed on to the nearest girder as the building shook for a moment.

"That . . . was . . . *awesome!*" Pyro whispered.

The three boys climbed down out of the window to the coolness outside. The sun was setting quickly now; there was barely any daylight left.

As soon as they had jumped into the bus, they grabbed the nearest seat. Reilly shut the door and struggled to put the bus in gear with a rusty grinding noise.

"Let's go!" Shields yelled.

The shift lever went into gear. Reilly yelled triumphantly, and he let out the clutch and stamped down on the gas pedal.

The bus lurched backward.

They were thrown from their seats as the rickety vehicle bumped over a curb and rammed the school's exterior brick wall. They stopped moving and the boys picked themselves up off the floor. Joey pushed Gerry off his shoulder, back to the window.

"Sorry about that," Reilly called, and set the shift into first gear. The bus bounced back over the curb.

Gerry groaned. "What . . . what the . . . ?"

"GO! GO! *GOOOOO!*" Shields screamed. He was pointing out the windows on one side.

Andy looked. There was a huge number of bugs bursting out of the building. "They must have thought that was an attack on the nest!" he cried.

Reilly looked into the mirror mounted on the side of the bus. He could see the creatures coming directly for the bus. "Whoa! *WHOA!*" he yelled, and stamped on the gas. The bus lurched forward.

Suddenly, the sky lit up. The school building was destroyed in a huge fireball, rising into the sky in a mushroom of flame.

"Hey, guys . . ." Hector began fearfully, but he never finished his thought. The bus was hit by the blast's shock wave.

They screamed as the rear of the bus was lifted off the ground. Reilly struggled to keep control of the front wheels as they were thrown forward.

The shock wave swept past them, and the bus's rear wheels hit the ground. Reilly stood on the brakes, and the bus shook as it skidded to a stop. They had been blown off the road and onto the packed dirt shoulder. The boys all looked at one another, wide-eyed.

"Can someone tell me what's going on?" a voice groaned. Gerry sat up, holding his head.

Reilly steered the bus back onto the road, and slowly, the bus built up speed.

From the back of the bus, Shields, Andy, and Pyro saw the flaming rubble of the school through the scratched emergency exit door. The flash from the blast had lit the desert up for a moment. Andy glanced over at Hector and Pyro. Eyes wide and glazed, Pyro stared at the flames. Hector looked briefly at him and shook his head, grinning. Hector gave Andy a silent thumbs-up.

In the sullen orange light cast by the flames, the boys could see silhouetted shapes moving toward them.

Andy squinted, trying to discern what they were. "What are those things?" he asked the others.

Pyro shook his head. It was too dark to make them out clearly. "They must be bugs. I see four of them, I think, maybe more. They're running."

The moon had risen, and once the smoke cleared a bit, they could see the creatures racing toward them like armored panthers.

"Man, those things are *fast*," Shields muttered. He turned and yelled toward the front of the bus. "Hey, Reilly . . . pick it up, they're coming after us!"

"I'm goin' as fast as I can!" Reilly shouted back. He didn't know if the bus could outrun the bugs for long. He glanced at the speedometer as it climbed toward sixty miles per hour. The temperature gauge was slowly inching toward "H." He decided not to mention it just now. He flicked the heater on full blast, sliding the temperature lever over to as hot as it would go. That would help to take some of the heat away from the engine. The

air blasting out from under the dashboard turned warm, then hot as the heater kicked in.

It's gonna be a race, he thought, *to see what happens first: Either the bugs catch up to us, or the engine overheats, and* then *the bugs catch us. Either way, we're dead.*

Andy, Shields, and Hector crowded
around the seat where Joey was helping Gerry to sit up. Gerry patted Joey on the shoulder. He winced when he touched the back of his head. "The last thing I remember, we were in the school, right?"

The boys went through the events that had occurred after Gerry had been knocked unconscious.

"Well, whadda we do now?" asked Shields as he walked down the center aisle of the bus after checking on Reilly, who was guiding the bus along the pitted road through the dark.

"We get to the nearest town and call the police," Gerry said grimly. "They'll have to call in the National Guard to blockade the area around the school. If any of those things get out, it'll be disastrous."

"Hey . . . hey, guys." Pyro's voice came from the rear of the bus. "I think we're in trouble."

Andy ran to the rear of the bus. The flames from the school provided enough light to see the swift forms closing in on the bus. "Faster! Go *faster*!" he yelled.

Shields ran back to the front of the bus and stood by Reilly as the bus slowly picked up speed again. It shuddered and shook as Reilly shifted gears. Shields opened his mouth to speak, but Reilly cut him off. "I know, I *know*! Faster!"

"Look at that," Gerry said as he joined Andy and Pyro at the back of the bus. "They're not running like insects. It looks like more of a cheetah-type stride. The leg arrangement on these creatures was altered to make them run more like a big cat."

The bugs loped toward them, steadily gaining ground on the bus as Reilly struggled to gain speed.

Pyro asked, "Hey, one of them jumped. Did you see?"

A metallic *thud* startled them as the bug landed on the roof of the bus. They could hear scraping sounds as it tried to bite through the metal of the roof.

Joey's voice quavered from one of the bus seats. "They . . . they can't get in, right?"

"No, no. Absolutely not," said Gerry. He thought for a moment. "I mean, unless they have been engineered with some kind of reinforced mandibles and expanded jaw musculature."

A sharp mandible drove through the bus roof with a metallic squeal. It worked back and forth, and opened a slice in the metal.

The bus shook as another bug vaulted onto the roof. It joined the first in starting to snip through the metal.

Glass sprayed into their faces as a soldier bug leaped onto the side of the bus, claws piercing the metal. It struck the windows with its huge head and jaws. Joey, sitting in the seat behind, pushed back into the cushions, too startled and frightened to move.

One of its legs reached inside and snagged Pyro's grimy T-shirt. He screamed as he was pulled to the side of the bus, the bug's jaws scrabbling and sliding against the window frame.

His screams reached Joey, who stared, frozen, as blood started soaking through Pyro's shirt. The bug's claws dug into his arm as he struggled to escape the thing's grip.

One of his hands, splashed with blood, struck Joey as he tried to pull himself away.

Deep inside Joey, something broke free; he had to do something and not let his fear paralyze him as it had all his life. He could *do something*, instead of standing by and waiting for someone else to tell him what he should do.

Andy had rushed over and was trying to pull Pyro away by his free arm, but that was only making the bug's claws dig in further. Its snapping mandibles were coming close to Pyro's head.

With a bellow, Joey got up and pushed Andy out of the way. He aimed a kick at the bug's leg that held Pyro pinned to the side of the bus. The leg cracked with a wet *snap*, and Pyro was free, screaming and holding his injured arm.

The bug didn't give up. It rammed its whole head through the window frame, antennae whipping about, trying to identify its enemy. Joey aimed a vicious kick at its head, breaking off an antenna. One more pushed it back out the window, and it lost its grip, falling away from the bus.

"Hey, somebody, help!" yelled Reilly from the driver's seat. One of the bugs was hanging from the roof, head-butting the windshield. The glass collapsed inward in a shower of tiny, glittering fragments.

Andy staggered to the front of the bus as it lurched on the road. He saw the Taser still in Reilly's back pocket as he wrestled with the steering wheel. Andy grabbed the Taser and rammed it into the bug's face, jabbing the activation button. The Taser flashed with a bright blue arc of light and a loud *zzzap*! The ant's head snapped back.

"Stop! *Stop the bus!*" Andy screamed in Reilly's ear.

Reilly slammed on the brake, and the bus shuddered to a halt, throwing the bug roughly off the hood and onto the blacktop road. Andy pulled Reilly out of the driver's seat.

Shields picked up a jar full of cesium sloshing around in oil from one of the boxes the boys had brought with them from the school. He lobbed it through the broken windshield. It shattered on the pavement between the bus and the bug.

"Everyone get down!" Gerry commanded.

The cesium exploded with a deafening *BOOM!* Sparks and bug parts blasted through the bus.

Reilly peeked out through the windshield frame. The bug had lost several legs on one side of its body and was crawling around in a circle, unable to move in a straight line.

He jumped back into the driver's seat and hit the gas. The bus rolled over the bug with a crunch. He whooped victoriously and started to drive again, but Gerry stopped him. He was propped against the front of the seat, holding his head weakly.

"Wait, wait . . . we have to get these two bugs off the bus." He pointed at the roof; the creatures were still snipping through the metal, attempting to peel the roof right off the bus.

He herded them all to the front of the bus. Hector and Pyro helped him up to a seat near the door. The bugs were becoming visible on the roof as they cut through more and more of the metal.

"All right, you guys, stay here and stay down!" he yelled. Gerry grabbed the last two jars filled with cesium and opened the bus door. Suddenly, he sagged dizzily back into the seat, the cesium jars clinking together.

Andy grabbed the jars out of Gerry's hands and ducked through the door before anyone could say a word.

He climbed out into the moonlit darkness. The cool air cleared his head. He ran a short way from the bus. The bugs saw his movement and jumped off the bus. He threw one jar of cesium, which shattered under one of them. There was a bright purple flash as the jar broke and detonated. Sparkling bits of glass sliced through Andy's T-shirt. The other bug was stunned, but recovered and started to run toward him. Andy waited until the last second, then dodged out of the creature's path. The bug skidded through the loose dirt as it tried to change direction. Andy threw his last cesium-filled jar as the thing opened its jaws in frustration. He heard the crack of glass as the jar broke open on the bug's serrated jaws. The cesium detonated as it mixed with the air in a violent, bright, smoky explosion. Big chunks of bug hit the ground as sparks fell around him.

Once his eyes readjusted to the dark, Andy carefully walked around the bus. The bugs were dead. He listened for any signs of more bugs following them, but he didn't hear anything.

Inside the bus, the boys and Gerry waited quietly. Pyro

opened the back emergency door and jumped down to the ground. He spotted Andy with his back to the bus, looking upward into the sky. Pyro opened his mouth to ask a question, but Andy held up a hand.

"*Shhh* . . . listen," he said quietly.

They could hear a humming sound. "What is that?" he asked.

Pyro pointed into the sky. There were some dark shapes moving across it. They glittered in the darkness. The humming was growing louder.

"Those must be the, um, eclosed princess bugs. I guess they weren't killed in the explosion. Their wings have hardened, and they're leaving to make new colonies."

One of the flying bugs passed right over them, fifty feet in the air. The humming of its wings raised the hairs on the back of Andy's neck. It was big. Light reflected from its veined wings flashed orange as it soared over-head and disappeared into the night.

"C'mon," Andy said, with a hand on Pyro's shoulder. "Let's get back to the bus, and get out of here." He shook his head. "No one's going to believe this."

They boarded the bus and started on the long road through the darkness to the nearest town.

13

ANDY STOOD MOTIONLESS, STARING OUT the window at the desolate New Mexico landscape. A cool breeze ruffled his hair as an air conditioner kicked on somewhere in the National Guard barracks offices. He studied the far-off scrubby hills, but didn't see any movement. The sun's glare made it hard to make out any detail, but he knew that the creatures were out there, somewhere. Tunneling, building.

"Andy? Andy Greenwood?" A woman's voice startled him. He turned and saw a middle-aged woman peeking out of a doorway along the hall. She gestured him into a small conference room, being used as an office. There were several stacks of folders full of papers on the table.

The woman picked up one folder, opened it, and sat down. Andy sat down across the table from her.

"Andy, my name is Jess Kaufman. I'm from Child Protective Services here in New Mexico. I wanted to talk to you for a few minutes and go through what happened to you and the other boys at the Reclamation School. Would you mind talking with me?" She pulled a yellow legal pad out of her briefcase and picked up a pen, jotting a couple of quick notes.

"Sure, I guess I can," Andy replied slowly.

It had been several days since the boys and Gerry had escaped from the school, and they were all still very strung out, jumping at the tiniest noises.

The events at the Reclamation School were still fresh in Andy's mind. He started with his arrival at the school, Switch's threat about extending the boys' stay, and suspicions that there were many more people involved in covering up the school's activities.

He continued on to the food fight, his punishment in the empty building, and the earthquake. Andy related Gerry's idea that what they thought was an earthquake was more likely another underground stash of chemicals that somehow was detonated by the tunneling of the bugs.

Andy had to stop several times as his emotions forced him to relive the horror of discovering the bugs and what must have happened to all the boys and teachers at the school. It was still almost as frightening in the retelling as it was when he was living through it.

Finally, he reached the point when they had escaped and blown up the school.

Gerry and the boys had rolled into a small police station in a little town after a six-hour drive through the cool New Mexico night.

The sergeant on duty was skeptical after hearing their horrific story until he stepped out into the night and saw the bus. His flashlight revealed shards of bug exoskeleton inside.

He phoned his captain, who phoned the state police. The state police called in the National Guard, who sent a squad of soldiers to check out the school, still skeptical of the wild story Gerry and the boys had told.

Ms. Kaufman related the details of what had happened next, based on conversations with soldiers around the barracks: A staff sergeant manning the communications equipment at the National Guard barracks had received an incoming transmission from the squad dispatched to check out the Reclamation School. They had come under attack by some kind of armored creatures emerging from the school, looking something like large insects. Several of the squad had been injured, and they were running out of ammunition rapidly.

The entire base was mobilized, with several trucks carrying soldiers racing to the unlucky squad's location, carrying heavy weapons and ammunition. Several helicopters buzzed into the sky and provided air support.

The fight was short. The disoriented and injured bugs weren't too difficult for the Guard to mop up, after they recovered from the shock of seeing tiger-sized, insectlike creatures coming at them. The soldiers contained the bugs and cordoned off the area around the school.

Twenty-four hours after the National Guard troops called in their report, three black Apache helicopters were patrolling the airspace above the destroyed school, like angry hornets. A large number of black, unmarked vans pulled up, and men dressed in black body armor entered the school. They emerged carrying bags and boxes from inside the school out to the vans.

Curious reporters were given only a vague story that an accident had happened at the school. The military and scientists being consulted needed time to formulate a strategy to deal with the creatures before their existence was revealed to the public. The reporters kept pushing, knowing that something big had happened. It was only a matter of time until they broke the story.

Andy and the boys were relieved to be housed temporarily at the National Guard barracks. They spent days being debriefed by government agents, who wrote down everything the boys said.

The soldiers at the base kept the boys busy when their presence wasn't required to describe their experiences to yet another government scientist. The boys were included in pickup basketball games, and were put to work helping to keep the barracks clean. Rather than being sullen about the positive, get-it-done attitude of the soldiers, the boys enjoyed it. After their recent harrowing experience at the doomed school, the structure of a military base was a welcome change.

After reaching the end of his story, Andy looked at Ms. Kaufman and said simply, "That's it."

Looking up from her notepad, Ms. Kaufman gave him a smile. "That's great, Andy. Thanks for your help." She looked over the notes she had taken and shook her head sadly. "After what you boys have told me about the way that the Reclamation School was being run, I can guarantee that there will be several arrests, including several police officials and at least one state judge."

Ms. Kaufman looked up at Andy. "A lot of people looked the other way on this, and they are going to be held accountable, you can be sure of that. As for those . . . creatures" — she shook her head — "that must have been horrifying. You should feel fortunate that you survived such an experience. I can't imagine what that must have been like."

She closed the file folder. "There is one more issue I'd like to talk to you about. There are a limited number of foster families in this area. It's going to take some time to locate a home to place you in.

"There is an option that I'd like you to consider. There has been one party who expressed interest in looking after you, at least on a temporary basis."

For a second, panic struck Andy. *She couldn't be talking about Chazz, could she?*

Ms. Kaufman picked up a typewritten note from Andy's file. "Dr. Medford submitted this to me. In it, he details how you, all of you, showed great bravery in an extremely difficult situation. He specifically mentioned your interest in the creatures, and your help during the whole situation.

"Dr. Medford is going to be stationed here for a time, studying the creatures further. He and his fiancée have offered to act as your legal guardians, at least until a more permanent situation can be set up for you. How does that sound to you?"

Andy laughed. "Well, yeah! That'd be . . . that'd be great!"

When he left the room, Andy found Hector and Pyro waiting for him in the hall. Pyro was jumping out of his skin.

"Dude, this is going to be so cool! We're all stayin' with Dr. Gerry!"

"Really? Awesome!" Andy said. "But what about your families?"

Pyro shrugged. "Hector's mom moved a few months ago, and nobody knows where. They're trying to track her down, but that's going to take some time. My parents said they won't take me back until they're sure I won't burn the place down."

"*I* sure wouldn't take you back," Hector said. He turned

to Andy. "You just missed Shields and Reilly. Child Protective Services said that Reilly's mom and dad are not ready for him to come back, so he can't go home yet, either. Shields's dad managed to get reassigned to the Camp Pendleton Marine base in California, and he said that Reilly could come and stay with them as long as he needed to. They're not leaving for another day or two, so we'll have the chance to say good-bye."

Gerry joined the boys, and clapped a hand on Andy's shoulder. "We're gonna see if we can track those bug princesses before they start new colonies. I just have to gather a little more gear, and we can go. Ever been camping?"

"The closest *I* ever got to camping was a field trip to the Santa Ana Zoo," Hector said.

"Well, what are we waiting around for?" Pyro yelled. "Let's *go*, already!"

EPILOGUE

THE PRINCESS FLEW AS FAST AS SHE could. The instinct to find the proper spot to start a colony was becoming strong. During her flight, she had transmitted scents into the air that would signal her location to any males following her.

She had flown during the cool night hours, several males performing aerobatic maneuvers around her to show their fitness as mates. She chose the strongest male to mate with, touching off the accelerated process that would produce eggs in a matter of days.

Finally, she had found a perfect spot: an empty house

in Nevada. She landed on the roof and sliced through papers stuck to the windows that read FORECLOSURE NOTICE and NOTICE OF EVICTION.

The interior of the house was dark, and what furniture and possessions had been left had been smashed. Vandals had broken all the windows in the house in the time since the former owners had left. All the houses for miles around were silent and abandoned. Whole blocks were empty and boarded up. No one had passed through the area for months. The only things moving were the signs that proclaimed HOUSE FOR SALE as they were buffeted by the hot desert wind.

There was plenty of room for the new colony to occupy.

The princess squeezed through a window frame and entered. She explored the house, and eventually found the way down to the basement. It was cooler down here, and would be a good place to breed new workers, soldiers, and sentries. She cleared a spot on the concrete floor and started depositing eggs. Each egg was covered with gooey slime, which she used to affix the eggs carefully to the cement walls. These would be the first of the workers, which would hatch and help her establish a new nest.

Very soon, she would be Queen.

THE END

TOP SECRET

NSDC SECURITY REGULATIONS APPLY

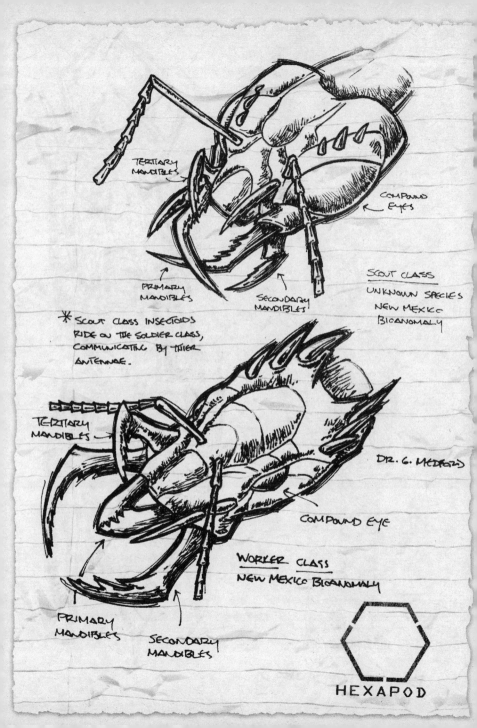

TERTIARY MANDIBLES

COMPOUND EYES

SCOUT CLASS

UNKNOWN SPECIES
NEW MEXICO
BIOANOMALY

PRIMARY MANDIBLES

SECONDARY MANDIBLES

✳ SCOUT CLASS INSECTOIDS
RIDE ON THE SOLDIER CLASS,
COMMUNICATING BY THEIR
ANTENNAE.

TERTIARY MANDIBLES

DR. G. MEDFORD

COMPOUND EYE

WORKER CLASS
NEW MEXICO BIOANOMALY

PRIMARY MANDIBLES

SECONDARY MANDIBLES

HEXAPOD

SOLDIER CLASS
NEW MEXICO BIOANOMALY

DR. G. MEDFORD

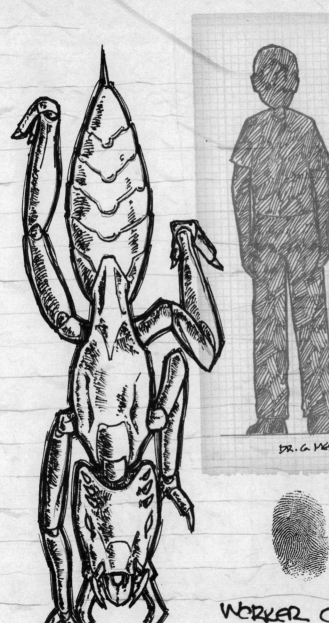

DR. G. MEDFORD

WORKER CLASS

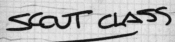

SCOUT CLASS

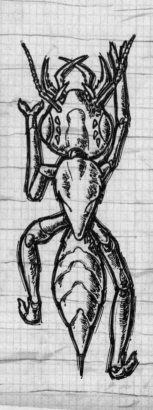

DR. G MEDFORD

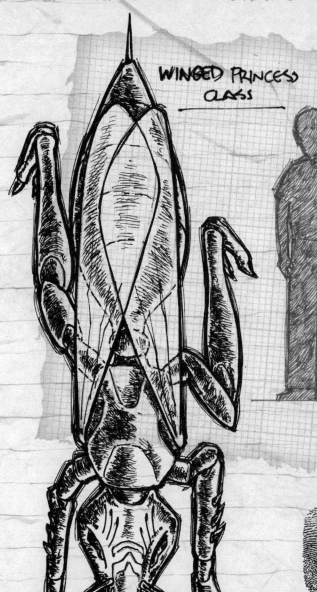

WINGED PRINCESS
CLASS

DR. G. MEDFORD

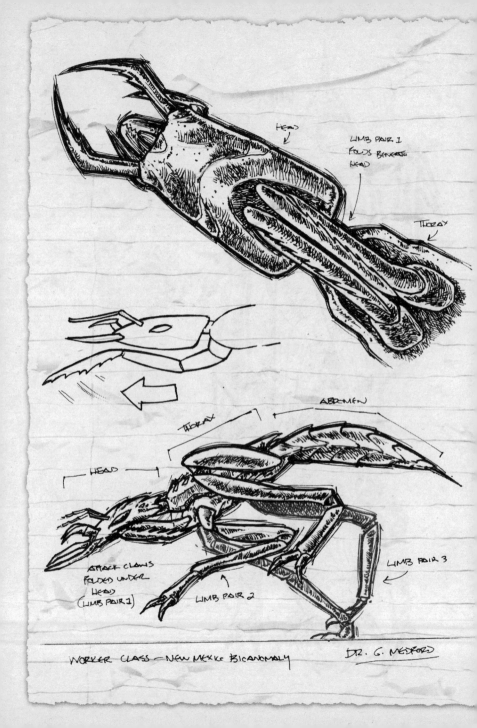

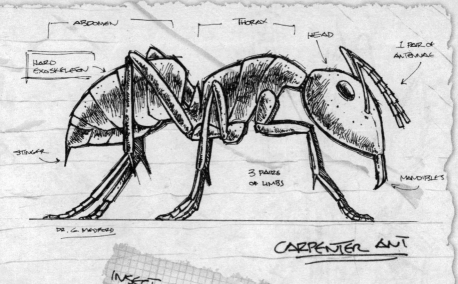

ABDOMEN

THORAX

HEAD

HARD
EXOSKELETON

1 PAIR OF
ANTENNAE

STINGER

3 PAIRS
OF LIMBS

MANDIBLES

DR. G. MEDFORD

CARPENTER ANT

INSECT CHARACTERISTICS
- 3 BODY SECTIONS
- 3 PAIRS OF LIMBS
- 1 PAIR OF ANTENNAE
- COMPOUND EYES

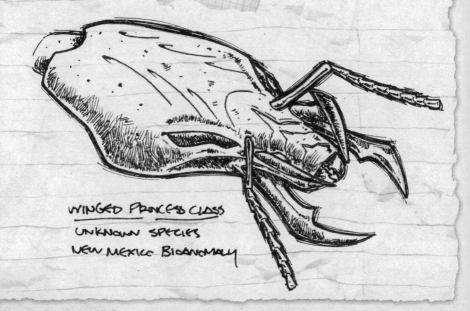

WINGED PRINCESS CLASS
UNKNOWN SPECIES
NEW MEXICO BIOANOMALY

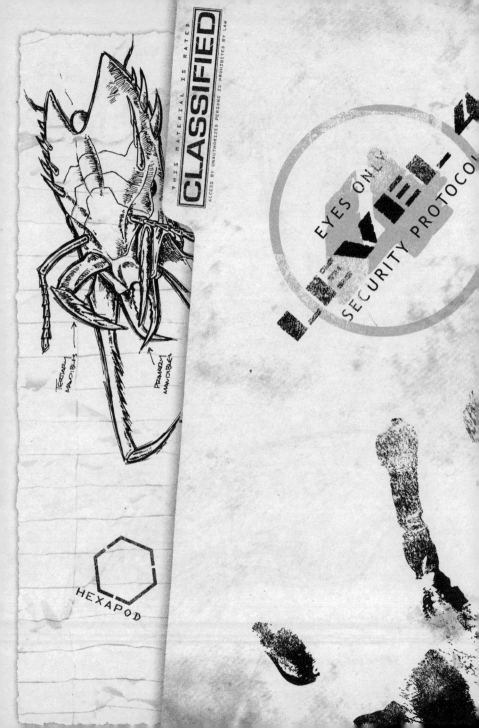

TERTIARY
MANDIBLES

PRIMARY
MANDIBLE

HEXAPOD